"We kissed...in b

Devlin's dark eyebrow quirked up and he grinned. "In bed," he confirmed. "It was very passionate."

Stunned, Carrie sat up and the sheet fell to her waist. With a soft cry, she snatched it up and tucked it up under her arms. "What else did I—I mean, we—do?"

He laughed. "I'm hurt. Usually I'm very memorable. In fact, most women want to relive the moment, again and again and—"

"I get the picture," Carrie muttered. How could she have slept through it all? Making love to her fantasy man and she couldn't remember a single moment of it. Unless... She cleared her throat. "Was I good?"

"Good? You were incredible. So passionate and uninhibited."

She ground her teeth. He was making fun of her. "That's amazing," she said in a soft voice. "Considering it was my first time. I always dreamed it would be perfect." She frowned. "I also thought I'd remember it."

His grin froze and his green eyes widened. "Your first time? You mean you're a..."

Carrie sighed dramatically. "Mmm-hmm. The first time I've ever—" she drew a deep breath and narrowed her eyes "—*ever met such a despicable, conceited, jerk!*"

Dear Reader,

With pages to write and deadlines to meet, it's always difficult to find time to schedule a real vacation. It seems I just finish one book and another hero and heroine are waiting for me to write their story. And when I do get away, my trips are usually for research and not for fun.

This year, I took a practical approach to vacations. I found a destination that required no air travel, no packing, no money. I decided to take my dream vacation in the pages of my manuscript. I had everything I needed—a warm climate, sunny beaches and a luxurious villa on a private island—even a gorgeous hero to do my bidding night and day. And I got a lot of writing done at the same time.

After I finished *Not in My Bed!*, I really felt like I'd been on a romantic getaway. I hope you feel that way, too.

Bon Voyage,

Kate Hoffmann

P.S. I love to hear from my readers! You can write to me c/o Harlequin Books, 225 Duncan Mill Road, Don Mills, Ontario, Canada, M3B 3K9.

NOT IN *MY* BED!
Kate Hoffmann

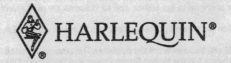

HARLEQUIN®

TORONTO • NEW YORK • LONDON
AMSTERDAM • PARIS • SYDNEY • HAMBURG
STOCKHOLM • ATHENS • TOKYO • MILAN • MADRID
PRAGUE • WARSAW • BUDAPEST • AUCKLAND

For Mary Bemis Raml, an old friend
who has become a new friend.

ISBN 0-373-25831-3

NOT IN *MY* BED!

Copyright © 1999 by Peggy Hoffmann.

Look us up on-line at: http://www.romance.net

Printed in U.S.A.

1

AN ICY LAKE WIND whipped down the main street of Lake Grove, sending a bone-deep chill through Carrie Reynolds's limbs and stinging her nose candy-apple red. As she approached the storefront building that housed her travel agency, Adventures, Inc., she glanced up at the colorful posters she'd placed in the windows in the hopes of luring new walk-in clients.

Fiji. An exotic island getaway…sugar-sand beaches…suntanned men, bodies glistening…and women in bikinis so tiny that they could double as dental floss.

Winter was always the worst. Four endless months of leaden skies and numbing cold, punctuated by a few sunny days. And the ever-present wind screaming in from Lake Michigan, turning Chicago and its northern suburbs into metropolitan Siberia. Though winter was bad for the mood, it certainly wasn't bad for business. As Carrie peered through the plate-glass window, she noticed at least three clients waiting to be helped. And another at Susie's—

"It's him," she murmured, her gaze drawn to the man sitting across from her partner, Susie Ellis. She'd recognize Dev Riley anywhere. Even through a frosted plate-glass window from twenty feet away with his back toward her and her glasses fogged up.

Carrie reached up to the bulky knit hat she'd tugged over her head before leaving the house. She hadn't even bothered with her hair that morning. And she'd skipped the makeup altogether. An oversize wool coat hid the worst of her sins: a dumpy green sweater and a pair of faded corduroys.

For a moment, she thought she might have time to run home and change. She only lived nine blocks away—a ten-minute walk if she rushed. But then Dev Riley stood up and shook Susie's hand. Before Carrie could formulate a new plan, he headed toward the front door, a familiar blue ticket folder clutched in his hand.

"Oh, God," she murmured, scanning the street for a place to hide. She pulled her hat down and her collar up, then spun around to cross the street. But the heel of her boot caught on an icy patch and, in a heartbeat, she lay sprawled on the sidewalk, her feet swept out from under her and a slow ache working its way from her derriere to her dignity.

Her hat had flown off and now tumbled down the sidewalk, blown by the wind. Her backpack lay near the curb, the bottle of grape juice she'd brought from home slowly seeping through the canvas to freeze in a purple puddle. And her glasses, knocked askew, had become tangled in her hair.

Carrie tried to scramble to her feet, but the lack of traction made the sidewalk treacherous. If she could just right herself, she might be able to—

"Are you all right?"

He had a voice exactly as she'd imagined: warm and rich, the kind of voice that could seduce with just a few simple words. Carrie had never heard him speak. Whenever he came into the agency, she always found some excuse to hide in the copy room or take refuge in the bathroom—any spot with a bird's-eye view. And considering that Devlin Riley traveled on business at least twice a month, she'd gotten quite adept at sprinting for cover and squinting through nearly closed doors.

"Can I help you?"

Carrie brushed the hair out of her eyes, knocking her glasses off in the process. Her breath froze as he held out his hand to her, long fingers gloved in elegant black leather. "No, thanks. I—I'm fine," she stammered.

"Please," he insisted, bending down and sending her a sympathetic smile. "Let me help you. Are you hurt?"

Carrie shook her head and was about to refuse his aid again, when he grabbed her hand and gently slipped his arm around her waist. An instant later, she was standing beside him, a slow flush of embarrassment warming her cold cheeks.

He was taller than she'd first imagined, his chin nearly even with her forehead. And his shoulders, emphasized by the fine cut of his cashmere overcoat, were impossibly broad. Carrie couldn't bear to look up into his eyes, but she just knew they were an intriguing shade of blue. She risked a glance—just one—but this time she couldn't look away.

"Green," she murmured beneath her breath. An

intriguing and unexpected shade of green. How could she have imagined them blue?

His dark eyebrow arched. "Green?"

Her gaze dropped to her mittened hand, which now clutched his arm. "Seen," she corrected, hesitantly drawing away. "I—I should have *seen* the ice."

He nodded, then bent down and retrieved her glasses. With careful hands, he replaced them, pushing them up on the bridge of her nose. "There, that should help."

"Thank you."

She watched as he grabbed her backpack, admiring the graceful way he moved, the way the wind ruffled his dark hair and the way the low morning light played over his perfect profile. "Gorgeous," she murmured.

Dev straightened and turned to her. "What?"

Carrie cursed inwardly. She had to learn to stop talking to herself! Living alone for the past eight years had turned her into a solitary chatterbox, giving voice to her every thought, just to fill her house with sound; carrying on extended philosophical conversations with her plants and her cat. "Gorgeous," she repeated, turning her face up to the gray sky. "I think it's going to be a gorgeous day."

He sent her another devastating smile, as she snatched the backpack out of his hands. "You think so? I heard it was supposed to snow. Five inches."

"I heard six," Carrie replied.

An uncomfortable silence grew between them, and though she wanted to drag her gaze away from his handsome face, she just couldn't. She wasn't sure when she'd get another chance to study him so openly. And looking at the real Dev Riley was so much better than her midnight fantasies and delicious daydreams.

He finally broke the stalemate, clearing his throat. "Well. If you're sure you're all right."

"I'm fine," Carrie said.

"Good. Then I'll be on my way." He gave her one last smile, then turned and headed down the sidewalk. She nearly sank to her knees in mortification, but then he turned back, and she quickly regained her composure. "You may want to stop in at the travel agency," he called, "and tell them about that icy sidewalk. They should put some salt down."

"I—I will!" Carrie cried, her voice cracking with forced enthusiasm. She hoisted her pack on her shoulder. "Yeah," she muttered. "I'll just walk right in and tell the owner what an idiot she is."

With a disgusted laugh, Carrie pulled open the front door and stepped inside. The warm interior fogged her glasses again, and when they cleared, she saw Susie standing in front of her. "You talked to him," she whispered. "You actually talked to Dev Riley." Susie shook her head in amazement. "I can't believe you finally worked up the courage. What did he say? What did you say?"

Carrie glanced at the waiting clients, then stepped around Susie and headed toward her desk. "I slipped, he helped me up, I thanked him. I looked like a complete klutz. Enough said."

She dropped her backpack beside her chair, then shrugged out of her coat and tossed her mittens aside. It was only then that she realized she'd lost her hat to the wind. "It was an ugly hat, anyway," Carrie muttered, avoiding her partner once again in her quest to get to the copy room and her morning coffee. "I need a doughnut."

High-fat bakery products always helped to soothe her nerves in the morning. French fries served as the tranquilizer of choice after eleven a.m. By late afternoon, she usually resorted to chocolate in any form. And before bed, there were those perfectly portioned pints of gourmet ice cream.

"I want to know what you said!" Susie cried, following hard on her heels. "You've been lusting after that guy for nearly two years, drooling and swooning every time he comes in the office."

"I never drooled!" Carrie said. "Now stop following me and go take care of your clients."

"I *am* taking care of my client—Dev Riley. Fantasy man. Hero of the hour."

Carrie groaned. There were times when she wished she'd remained a sole proprietorship. But Adventures, Inc. had grown too successful for one person to handle all alone. So Susie had gone from indispensable travel agent to aspiring partner, gradually buying into an equal share of the business. And along the way, she'd become Carrie's best friend—and tormentor.

In return, Carrie had been relieved of most of the more distasteful duties of a travel agent—like travel, for instance. Susie had also nagged and interrogated and lectured about her personal life until she had absolutely no secrets left anymore. "I don't lust after Dev Riley," she murmured as she poured herself a cup of coffee. "I admire his..."

Carrie struggled for a word. His face? His body? His easy charm and smile? "His coat," she finished. "I—I think he has a wonderful fashion sense." She glanced up at Susie. "It was cashmere."

"And you couldn't be a worse liar." Susie studied Carrie thoughtfully. "Actually, it's good you finally talked to him. This is a big step for you. We both know, it's time you got a life. A real life with a real man."

Carrie took a bite of her doughnut. "I have a life," she said, her mouth full.

"You have a career," Susie corrected. She leaned against the counter. "You and I both know that you haven't had a life of your own since you were ten years old."

Susie was right. Carrie's life had been an idyllic picture of childhood happiness until her mother died almost twenty years ago. After that, as an only child, Carrie had become the woman of the house. She had cooked for her father and cleaned the house, ironed and shopped. And when she wasn't doing that, she lost herself in schoolwork. A straight-A student, Carin Louise Reynolds was the only person in the history of Lake Grove High School to win the geography prize four years in a row.

When it came time for college, she had turned down an academic scholarship at a prestigious east coast university, and chosen a small college within a half-hour drive of home. She didn't really mind caring for her father. Carrie loved him more than anyone, and enjoyed being needed. And it always gave her an excuse to avoid all the social pitfalls

that came with high school: dates and dances...
boys. She had to do the wash or pay the bills or iron
her father's shirts for the next week.

In fact, she'd nearly resigned herself to a rather
sedate future as a geography teacher, when her father did something completely out of character.
The week of her college graduation, John Reynolds
proudly announced his retirement, bought a condo
in Florida, turned the deed for their house over to
her, and presented her with a check for ten-
thousand dollars. Basically, he told her that it was
time for both of them to get a life.

So she had bought a little travel agency located
in the quaint business district of Lake Grove, a
pretty bedroom suburb of Chicago filled with old
brick houses on tree-shaded streets and populated
with lots of disposable income. She created a niche
for herself by booking adventure travel—trekking
trips to the Himalayas, rafting trips down the Am-
azon, climbing expeditions to Antarctica—unique
trips. It had brought in a young, upscale clientele
and had been the key to Adventure, Inc.'s ever-
increasing profits.

"Carrie?"

She looked at Susie and forced a smile, her mind
already on a recent drop in airfare commissions
and the effect on the bottom line. "I plan to get a
life," she murmured. "I really do. Just as soon as I
have time."

"Well, I suggest you begin this morning," Susie
said, leaning forward. "You spoke to Dev Riley,
your ultimate fantasy man. Now I think you
should take the next step."

"The next step?"

"Call him up. Ask him out on a date. Lunch would be good. A little thank-you for picking you up off the sidewalk. I've got his number."

"He has a girlfriend. Isn't that what you told me? Besides, why would he ever accept a lunch invitation from me?" There was no use deluding herself. Dev Riley would never be attracted to her—a slightly klutzy, socially inept introvert with thick glasses and a perm from hell. She had a better chance of winning the Illinois lottery.

She glanced at her reflection in the coffeemaker, then ran her fingers through her tangled hair. Had she taken more care with her appearance this morning, she might have felt differently. But Carrie had always dressed in a fashion that made her nearly invisible to the opposite sex. Perhaps it was a way to protect herself, to rationalize any rejection she might experience. Of course men weren't attracted to her. Why would they be? "I couldn't," she murmured.

"You never know unless you try," Susie said.

Nervously, Carrie pushed her glasses up the bridge of her nose; powdered sugar from her doughnut smudged the lenses . "He'd say no."

Susie stood up. "Maybe he wouldn't."

"Oh, right. I'd be a welcome change from the gorgeous women he probably dates. From fashion models to flabby thighs. *Now* who's living in a fantasy world?" Carrie sighed.

"If you wait too long, you'll miss your chance," Susie warned.

"What is that supposed to mean?"

She smiled sympathetically. "I just planned a romantic vacation for two for him. He was here to pick up the tickets. This is the first vacation he's ever had me plan—it's always business trips. But this time, he led me to believe that he was about to pop the question to his traveling companion. Her name is Jillian. Jillian Morgan."

The name was like a knife to Carrie's heart. "He—he's getting married?" She turned away and tried to quell the unbidden flood of emotion that surged up inside of her. How could she feel this way about a man she didn't even know? He was nothing to her—just a silly fantasy! He barely even knew she was alive.

She took a shaky breath. "Let's be practical. A guy like Dev Riley would never look twice at me. Besides, I made a fool of myself out there. I could barely put two words together. I just can't talk to men."

Susie patted her on the shoulder. "Making a fool of yourself is part of life—and love. We all do it." She paused. "You just seem to do it more often than most people, but that's part of your charm."

"My charm?"

"Carrie, you run one of the most successful travel agencies in the metro area. You're a well-respected businesswoman. You're smart and funny. And you're pretty, too, if you'd only pay a little attention to your appearance."

"I'm also the most boring person you know," Carrie countered. "What's worse, I'm the most boring person *I* know!"

Susie paused. "Well, you can change that. Every day, you plan exotic adventure vacations for your clients. And yet, you've never really had an adventure—or a vacation—yourself."

Carrie frowned, sipping her coffee. "Traveling alone always seems so...desperate. So pitiful." She drew a deep breath. "And a little frightening."

"Then let me plan a vacation for you," Susie suggested. "I'll make all the arrangements. I guarantee, when you come back, you'll be a different person."

"I don't know, I—"

"Do it! Take the first step. I promise, you won't regret it."

Carrie took another bite of her doughnut. Susie was right. How could she expect a man like Dev Riley to find her interesting when she didn't find herself interesting? He traveled the world. She read travel brochures. He lived life, and she merely stood on the sidelines and observed. He had sex on a regular basis. She managed an intimate encounter with a man about as often as the nation elected a new president.

Maybe she did need to shake up her life a little. She was nearly thirty years old, and she'd spent the last year mooning over a man she could never have. It was time to step out of her safe little world and take a chance. There had to be at least one other man like Dev Riley out there...waiting for the woman of his dreams.

"So what's it going to be, Carrie Reynolds? Need I remind you that you turn thirty in two months? The world is waiting, and you're just getting older."

"I'll think about it," Carrie replied. "I'll let you know."

"This morning?"

"This week."

"Today," Susie insisted. "The rest of your life begins today! If you aren't on a plane by the end of this week, I'm giving up on you!"

Susie strode out of the copy room, leaving Carrie to consider her suggestion. To be honest, she'd been working on a few changes in her life. The perm from hell had been the first step in that direction—a spontaneous decision she had come to regret. She had really been thinking about a new coat of paint for the house or maybe a new car, but the pretty picture in the beauty shop window had muddled her common sense. In a secret corner of her heart, she had hoped that a new hairstyle might give her a boost in confidence, might make her more attractive to the opposite sex.

If she really wanted a man like Dev Riley—a relationship that was more than just a silly dream—then she'd have to turn herself into the type of woman he'd want. An adventurous, confident, worldly woman. A woman who could talk about more than just airfare wars, and group discount rates on hotels, and liability concerns for rental cars. A woman who didn't stuff herself with doughnuts every time she felt depressed.

"I'll do it," Carrie murmured, tossing her doughnut into the trash. "I'll do it! Or I'll make a fool of myself trying."

BY THE TIME THE TAXI pulled up to Carrie's resort, she was ready for a nap. The flight to Miami had been a white-knuckle affair. It was only the third time Carrie had been on a plane in her life. She had clutched the airsickness bag to her chest from takeoff to landing, and had tried to keep her mind off her nausea by focussing on Serendipity, the luxurious singles resort that Susie had booked for her.

It had taken a few days of cajoling, but she'd finally agreed with Susie's choice of destination. What better way to test the social waters? her partner had urged. There'd be plenty of available men to practice on, group activities that might mask her shy nature, and a relaxed atmosphere that was guaranteed to put her nerves at ease.

Carrie had studied so many travel brochures over the years that she could picture it so clearly: palm trees swaying in the south Florida breeze, the sound of the ocean, a balcony that overlooked the beach, a huge comfortable bed and a staff ready to cater to her every whim. She'd exercise and eat healthy food and pamper herself.

And maybe she'd venture out of her room once or twice to survey the singles crowd. She'd have to collect a few good stories to bring home, a few handsome men to describe, a few conversations to recount. Carrie moaned softly. Maybe it wasn't the travel that was making her nauseated, but the prospect of real social interaction with the opposite sex.

Or maybe it was the high-speed cab ride from the airport, weaving through traffic and tossing her around in the wide back seat. When she finally stepped out of the stifling car into the Miami heat and humidity, her knees nearly buckled beneath her. "There's a good reason I don't travel," she murmured, adjusting the straw hat on her throbbing head.

Airsickness, carsickness, a general sense of being out of control and out of her element. Visiting new and exciting places was now accompanied by the threat of another visit—from her last meal. If she could just conquer her nerves, she'd be fine.

The cabbie grabbed her bags from the trunk and set them beside her. Carrie rubbed her tired eyes, then looked around for a bellman. But there wasn't a bellman in sight…probably because there wasn't a resort in sight. They were parked at the water-front, at the entrance to a brightly lit marina. "This isn't the Serendipity. There's supposed to be a re-sort, with lots of single—rooms."

The cabbie glanced at his clipboard. "This is it," he said. "This is the address you gave me. This is the Miamarina."

She turned to scan the opposite side of the street. "But there's no resort here. There must be some mistake."

The driver shrugged and pointed toward the fence. "There's a sign over there on the fence that says *Serendipity*. Maybe that's a boat to the resort?"

Carrie groaned and slowly lowered herself onto her pile of luggage. "Oh, no. Not a boat. The plane was bad enough. I'm not getting on a boat."

"Well, lady, I have another airport run to make," the cabbie said. "I can take you back to Miami International, or you can stay here. Your choice."

Carrie gnawed on her lower lip. She'd come this far in the name of adventure. She couldn't quit now, defeated by a measly little boat ride. Susie would never let her forget it. "Go on. I'll be fine," she said, waving him off.

The taxi roared away, and Carrie cupped her chin in her hand and sighed. So much for her lux-urious getaway. She was sick, she was hot, she had a splitting headache, and now, she had to get on a boat before she could even hope to take a shower and a nap. If most people handled travel as poorly as she did, Carrie realized, she'd be out of business pretty quickly. "People love to travel," she assured herself. "It's supposed to be fun. I'm having fun."

Carrie ran her fingers through her hair, then winced at the tangles. She'd spent most of the past three days getting primped and prettied for her big adventure. Her mousy-brown hair had been lightened to a sunny shade of blond and cut in an attractive shoulder-length bob. The girls at the salon had plucked her brows and pinched her cheeks, and when she left, she'd barely recognized herself.

She'd passed an entire day with Susie in a mad shopping spree at Watertower Place. They spent hundreds of dollars on fashionable warm weather wear, then went to Susie's condo and packed it all up in her partner's designer luggage, after adding a few choice items from Susie's wardrobe.

Carrie rubbed her eyes again. She'd even dug up the contact lenses she'd tried last year, hoping to show off the blue eyes that her hairdresser called "marvelous." But she knew better. All the stylists and best friends in the world would never be able to convince her that she was drop-dead gorgeous.

She was far too curvy to be fashionable. And too short to be considered statuesque. Her hair vacillated between mildly temperamental and downright belligerent. And her features were rather plain. All and all, she was what most men would consider ordinary—if a man ever took the time to consider her at all.

Maybe she was to blame for that. She always

thought that when the right man came along, he'd recognize her positive attributes, and they'd live happily ever after. But after her silly infatuation with Dev Riley, she had been forced to conclude that if she ever wanted a chance at love and marriage, she'd have to make a few changes in her life. She'd have to stop hiding inside plain clothes and behind thick glasses. She'd have to learn to be charming and witty, to act confident even when she wasn't.

That's what this vacation was. A trial run in a place where she wouldn't have to risk running into someone she knew. She could make all her mistakes, swallow all her fears and confront all her insecurities. And when she went back home, maybe her life would become more than just her job.

"Ahoy there!"

Carrie looked up and saw a white-haired man, dressed in creased white shorts, a white shirt and a neat white cap, standing at the gate into the marina. He stood next to a cart loaded with coolers. An ice-cream vendor. God, she could go for an ice-cream cone right now. Maybe she'd have two, since her nerves were particularly frayed.

"Would you be Miss Reynolds, then?"

She shaded her eyes against the glare from his uniform. How would an ice-cream vendor know her name? Her stomach lurched. Right now, she really didn't care. Rocky road was all she could think about. Or maybe butter pecan.

"I'm Captain Fergus O'Malley," he said as he approached, his words thick with an Irish accent. He was a sturdy man with thick white eyebrows that nearly obscured his eyes. His skin was nut-brown and leathery from the sun, and though he was a complete stranger, Carrie immediately knew he'd be sympathetic to her plight.

"Captain Fergus?" She drew in a deep breath and wobbled to her feet. "Captain Fergus, do you have chocolate mint? Or rocky road? I'd even settle for plain old strawberry. Two scoops on a sugar cone."

A smile creased his weather-worn face. "Ice cream, is it? I can see what we have on board *Serendipity*, miss."

She frowned. Was this man sent to take her to the resort? "On *board Serendipity*? Don't you mean *at*?"

"No. On the boat. I'm Captain Fergus O'Malley, captain of *Serendipity*. And I'll wager you'd be one of my passengers: Carin Reynolds. Let me grab your bags, and I'll take you on board. Get you settled in."

"On board," Carrie murmured. "Then—then you aren't an ice-cream vendor? And Serendipity isn't a beautiful resort with soft beds and hot showers?" *And handsome single men*, she added silently, *in skimpy swimsuits*.

Captain Fergus chuckled as if she'd made a joke, and set off with her luggage tucked beneath his arms. "*Serendipity* is a fifty-four-foot ketch, one of the most luxurious bluewater boats to sail the Caribbean. We have a soft bed and a hot shower for you—that we do. And gourmet meals and fine wines. Did you not look at our brochure?"

Carrie shook her head and trailed along behind him, her legs feeling like limp linguini. "This whole vacation was supposed to be an adventure.

The plane ride was an adventure and the taxi from the airport was an adventure. But a sailboat? That's too much adventure for me. You see, I'm not a strong swimmer and, I always say, if you don't want to drown, stay away from water. But that would be a little hard to do on a sailboat, don't you think?"

"There's no need to worry about your safety. And we won't be at sea all the time. We'll be putting in at pretty little spots almost daily, all along the Florida Keys."

She rubbed her throbbing temples. "But how am I supposed to practice?" she mumbled. "Susie knew I wanted to practice. Why would she put me on a sailboat where there's no one to practice with?"

"Practice?" Captain Fergus asked, stopping to look back at her. "And what would you be wantin' to practice?"

Carrie shook her head. "Never mind." She glanced up at the dock, a wave of nausea hitting her at the sight of the rocking sailboat. Carrie swallowed hard. "I'm going to kill you, Susie Ellis. I swear, as soon as I get home, you're going to pay for this."

"Well, here she is. I hope you'll have a fine voyage with us, Miss Reynolds."

"I'm sure I would have a fine time, if I were to get on your boat. But I can't. I'm afraid I'd get...ill."

Captain Fergus hoisted her luggage on board. "We can take care of that right away. You just wait there, and I'll get you some sea-sick pills. It'll set you to rights in a jiffy."

Carrie forced a smile. "That would be nice. I'll just sit here on this nice bench and contemplate my future. And the imminent murder of my business partner."

Captain Fergus gave her an odd look, then hopped on board and disappeared into the cabin. He returned a few minutes later with a huge fruit drink and a bottle of pills. "A welcome refreshment," he said. "No alcohol, but it will help wash the medicine down. You'll become accustomed to the motion after a short time. In a few days, you won't even notice it."

Captain Fergus proved to be right about the accommodations. After a half hour on the pier, Carrie managed to venture on board *Serendipity*, and found it all the captain had claimed. Her cabin was large and luxurious, with a huge sitting area that the captain called the "main saloon" and an equally large bedroom that he called the "forward berth." Even the tiny bathroom had a special name: the "head." *Serendipity* boasted all the amenities one would find in a fine hotel—except other guests.

Once she'd settled in, the first mate and chef—Captain Fergus's lovely wife, Moira—brought her a small tray of fresh fruit and a lobster salad, which she gobbled down.

As the sun began to set, the air grew still in the cabin, and Carrie grew drowsy. Her clothes clung to her sticky skin, and she stripped them off, anxious to wash away the remains of a hectic day from her body and her mind. Wrapped in a towel, she headed for the bathroom. But she couldn't muster the energy to step inside the tiny coffin that served as a shower.

With a sigh, she returned to her cabin, tossed aside the towel and climbed into bed, too exhausted to search her bags for a nightgown. The crisp cotton sheets felt deliciously cool on her skin, and the medicine gave her a pleasant sense of lethargy.

Carrie had never gone to bed without her pajamas, but she was just going to lie down for a short nap. She was alone; what harm could it do? After a few hours' sleep, she'd get up, find a phone, call Susie and insist that she book a *real* vacation—in a hotel that didn't rock and creak and threaten to make her lose her lunch.

The gentle motion of the boat against the dock gradually lulled her into a deep sleep, the sound of the water against the hull soothing her ragged nerves. She awoke once and wondered where she was, but then allowed herself to drift back into a hazy dreamworld, satisfied that she was safe...and comfortable and...

The fantasy was not new. Dev Riley had invaded her dreams many times before. But he had always been a vague and unfocused presence. This dream was different. This time, he came alive in her imagination—the sound of his voice, the color of his eyes, the heady scent of his cologne.

Carrie sighed softly and wrapped her arms around a fluffy down pillow, stretching her naked body beneath the sheets. Dreaming of Dev was a wonderful vacation all its own. In her dreams, she was pretty and clever and sexy—exactly the type of woman a man like Dev Riley preferred. And he was passionate and commanding and completely enchanted by her charms.

They were in his bedroom—one of her favorite versions of the dream. He had a huge bed with filmy fabric draped like a canopy around them. Candles flickered in the darkness, bathing the room and his naked chest in golden light. He knelt over her, watching, waiting, the muscles in his shoulders and chest bunching and flexing, his hand hovering just inches from her skin....

But the bedroom dream never went any further. They never kissed or spoke; they simply watched each other...and waited. Carrie moaned and clutched the pillow in her fists.

Why did the dream always stall right before it really got good?

2

DEV RILEY WAS LATE. He'd nearly canceled this trip, but at the last minute, decided to go ahead with his plans anyway. To hell with Jillian Morgan! For that matter, to hell with women in general. It would be a cold day in the Florida Keys before he put his heart on the line again, before he trusted his future to a fickle female.

This trip was supposed to mark a turning point in his life. He'd been dating Jillian for nearly two years, and marriage had been the next logical step. Dev hadn't come to that conclusion without considerable thought. He'd weighed the pros and cons of a lifelong commitment and had decided to proceed.

After all, Jillian was beautiful, confident, intelligent, independent—the type of woman he'd be proud to call his wife. She loved her job, but more important, she understood his own obsession with work—the long hours and the late nights. And marrying Jillian was preferable to trying to find another woman who accepted his hectic life-style and his reluctance to start a family. Besides, he and Jillian spent most of their limited free time together. Why not make it official?

He'd given his travel agent a blank check. "Plan the most romantic getaway you can think of," he'd told Susie Ellis. "We want to be alone." And then he had surprised Jillian with the tickets. At first, she'd stubbornly refused to accompany him, begging off with excuses about work. But he'd worn her down, and finally she'd agreed that a vacation was precisely what they needed.

A bitter laugh burst from his lips. He'd been stupid enough to believe that Jillian had shared his plans for the future—until two days ago. He'd come home to find her gone—all her clothes and possessions missing—as if she'd never come into his life at all. He'd found a note of explanation, a businesslike missive—a resignation letter, of sorts—explaining that she'd decided to accept a promotion at work. A promotion that involved an immediate move to New York.

That news was followed by her sincerest wishes for his happiness. She'd wanted to break the news to him on their vacation, but then thought better of it. Never once had she mentioned love or commitment. Nor had she expressed any regret for her sudden decision. The words that she'd so blithely uttered during their moments of passion had meant nothing to Jillian, especially when they stood in the way of her precious career.

Dev slouched down and watched the lights of Miami's waterfront through the tinted limo window. Hell, even he'd been so obsessed with work, he'd chosen a destination that was just a short plane ride away from Chicago. He could have taken Jillian to Paris or Rome, but he'd thought about business first. He'd been a fool to think they could have a future together. The only common interest they shared—the single-minded pursuit of professional success—had doomed them from the start. But if he couldn't build a future with a woman like Jillian, who was left?

Maybe no one, Dev mused. Maybe he was destined to remain a bachelor for the rest of his life. All things considered, it wasn't a bad option. After all, he'd never had any problems getting a date when he needed one. And when a woman became too demanding of his time and energy, he'd just cut her loose and move on. He could go back to that life as easily as he'd planned to move forward into marriage, couldn't he?

Dev rubbed his forehead with his fingertips, trying to quell an ache growing there. So, that was the way his life would be. From now on, he was on his own. Women would have just one place in his world and that would be in his bed—on his terms! Once he got back from vacation, he'd throw himself into his work. But until then, he'd spend this next week alone, putting the bitter memories of Jillian into proper perspective. Putting women out of his life for good.

He'd learn the ins and outs of sailing. He'd get plenty of clean air and sunshine. He'd do a little snorkeling. He'd sleep late and waste time and teach himself to relax. And when he got home, his affair with Jillian would have become a distant memory.

The limo came to a stop at the entrance to the marina. As the driver opened the door, Dev could hear the clank of the rigging and the sound of water slapping against the sides of the yachts moored at the docks. Tall masts rocked back and forth against the night sky, creating wavering shadows on the sidewalk.

For a brief moment, he thought about asking the driver to take him back to the airport. This trip could turn out to be an excruciating bore—long days on the water, the only respite from sailing a private island retreat where he'd enjoy luxurious solitude...guaranteed to drive him crazy. And he could better use the time at the office, planning his next acquisition, while blotting the mistake called "Jillian" from his mind.

He'd never taken a real vacation—one that included complete isolation and relaxation. A few days off here and there were all he could spare, and he usually took his work along. "Come on, Dev," he muttered to himself. "You run a multinational corporation. Surely you can handle a vacation by yourself. It's time you learned to chill out."

What was he afraid of? Too much time to think? Too much time to examine the choices he'd made in his life? The mistakes? Too much time to get to know the man he'd become? He was thirty-seven years old. By this age, he should be comfortable in his skin. But since he'd taken over his father's business fifteen years ago, Dev had spent his days immersed in responsibility, loving every minute of it. It was only in the quiet moments of his day that he wondered whether there wasn't more to life than what he had.

With a soft curse, Dev stepped out of the limo and grabbed his bag from the driver. This was no time to examine his faults. A vacation was meant to be fun! He crossed to the gate and nodded at a uniformed man who waited there, warned of his arrival by a call from the airport. "Sorry to be so late," he murmured.

The captain smiled. "You'd be on vacation now, Mr. Riley. We don't watch clocks here."

Dev chuckled. "I'll try to remember that, Mr...."

"Captain Fergus," the older man replied with a thick brogue. "We're ready to cast off as soon as you're on board. Your companion arrived late this afternoon, and she's settled into your cabin."

Dev stopped on the pier and stared at the captain. "My companion?"

"She had a little problem with seasickness, but we took care of that. I believe she's asleep now. A pretty young lady, she is."

"My companion," Dev repeated. He drew a deep breath and let it out slowly. So Jillian had changed her mind. Her note had seemed so final. He'd canceled her half of the trip with his travel agent, and hadn't decided to go himself until a few hours before his flight took off.

If she'd had second thoughts, why hadn't she called him? Why just turn up in Miami without a word? Perhaps she didn't want to give him a chance to refuse her. Maybe she wanted the opportunity to apologize, to set things right. Dev sighed softly. Was he willing to forgive her? Could he ever trust her again?

"Would you care for some dinner, Mr. Riley? Perhaps a drink before we set sail."

Dev looked at his watch. It was nearly midnight. "Set sail? Now?"

"We sail at night so that you'll have your days for sightseeing. I know these waters like the back of my hand. No need to worry. With satellite navigation, it's no problem."

He shook his head wearily. "I think I'd like to get some sleep. You can take off right away. I'm sorry I held us up."

The captain showed Dev into the main saloon, then pointed down a companionway. "Your berth is forward. There's a tiny berth next to the head where you can store your luggage. We'll be in Elliott Key by early morning. You can have lunch on shore if you like."

"Great," Dev said without much enthusiasm. He wasn't even sure if he and Jillian would be speaking to each other by the next day, much less sharing a meal. Her sudden desertion spoke volumes about her feelings for him—feelings that he intended to fully understand before they docked tomorrow. "I'll see you in the morning, Captain."

The cabin was dark when Dev stepped inside; the only light was that filtering through the row of portholes on either side of the bed. He reached for the switch, then paused before drawing his hand away. He really didn't want to talk to Jillian right now. His mind had been dulled by the effects of a long day of travel, and he wasn't in the mood for an argument.

With a deep sigh, he dropped his bags on the floor and shrugged out of his jacket. He'd wait and confront her tomorrow morning, when he felt sharper and his resolve was more focused. As Dev stripped down to his boxers, he stared at the unmoving form curled beneath the covers.

He fought a sudden urge to do away with the boxers and crawl in beside her, waking her slowly with his mouth and his hands. Perhaps if he made love to her first, he'd forget all his anger, and they'd be able to pass a tolerable vacation together. They'd always been good together, sharing a rather reserved passion in bed that they both found satisfying. And at the end of the vacation, they would go their separate ways. By that time, he'd have convinced himself not to care one way or the other.

In the end, Dev stretched out on top of the covers, folding his arms behind his head. He'd settled on spending this vacation in solitary pursuits, and was even looking forward to some time alone. Now, he rather resented Jillian's presence. "It wouldn't be such a bad thing to be without a woman," he murmured, glancing over at her. "At least for a little while."

Jillian moaned softly, and he felt her press against him. Dev clenched his teeth and fought his impulses. So much for good intentions. Though he didn't want to wake her, just how was he supposed to resist her warm body curled against his, her breath soft against his bare skin? He turned toward her and stroked her cheek, her skin like warm silk.

With a groan, he slid down beside her and drew her body against his. His mouth found hers in the darkness, and he kissed her. For a brief instant, he hesitated, doubt niggling at his mind. She felt different in his arms, tasted different. His fingers tangled in her hair, and he wondered when she'd decided to curl it.

He brushed his thoughts aside as easily as he brushed the sheet from her body. Slowly, his hands found familiar flesh…familiar, yet unfamiliar to his touch. Where he once caressed hard muscle, he now enjoyed soft curves. The sweet fragrance of her perfume drifted around him as he bent to kiss her breast. Even her perfume smelled different...exotic...arousing.

"Mmm," she murmured, arching against him. "You're here. You're really here."

Dev froze at the sound of her voice, then pulled away. Stunned, he reached out and flipped on the bedside light, then looked down at the naked woman lying beside him. Her face was tipped up to the light, but her eyes were still closed. For an instant, Dev thought he recognized her, but then he realized the woman in his cabin—in his bed—was a complete stranger!

With a curse, he grabbed the sheet and carefully arranged it over her naked body. When his heart had stopped pounding and he'd gained control of his senses, Dev he reached out and grasped her shoulders. He gave her a gentle shake, but she didn't open her eyes. Then he scrambled out of bed and stood above her, not sure what propriety dictated in a situation like this. It certainly didn't allow for the growing desire evident beneath his boxer shorts.

Dev grabbed his trousers and tugged them on, leaving the button unfastened at his waist. Had another passenger stumbled into his cabin by mistake? He shook his head. That couldn't be! He and Jillian were to be the only passengers on *Serendipity*. That left only a member of the crew. He bent down and studied her face. For a person who spent her days on a sailboat, she was remarkably pale.

No, she couldn't be part of the crew. Captain

Fergus had called her his "companion." Then
what? She could have stowed away on this boat
under false pretenses, claiming his bed as her own.
Dev frowned. Who was she? And what the hell
was she doing in his bed? Surely she wasn't one of
the amenities that this charter offered!

He reached out to touch her again, then drew his
hand away. She had the most incredibly soft skin,
like nothing he'd ever touched before. Dev knelt
down and studied her at eye level, his chin resting
on his fist, his brow furrowed. On first glance, she
wasn't what he'd consider beautiful. But upon
more careful consideration, Dev had to admit that
the woman in his bed was intriguing.

The differences between this woman and Jillian
were like those between night and day. Jillian was
cool and inaccessible. Her willowy body had been
meticulously sculpted by a personal trainer, and
she possessed a worldly attitude that came with
the knowledge that her dark beauty was matched
only by her intelligence and drive.

In contrast, this woman was all sunshine and
light, from her curly blond hair to her fresh-faced
looks. A scattering of freckles dusted her upturned
nose and her pale cheeks. Her wide, lush mouth
was curled up in what Dev suspected was a per-
manently impish smile. And from the curves that
he could see hidden beneath the sheet, he doubted
that she spent a lot of time pumping weights at her
local gym.

She was everything that he'd never been attracted to. Yet Dev couldn't seem to take his eyes
off her, couldn't shake the feeling that he somehow knew her. A cool salt-tinged breeze drifted

through the cabin from the open hatch, and he watched as it fluttered a strand of her hair.

A sensible man would shake her awake and demand an explanation. A proper gentleman would at least search out the captain and find out how a stranger had ended up in his cabin. But Dev Riley was neither sensible nor a gentleman. Instead, he decided to crawl back into bed and get some sleep.

He would find out soon enough who this woman was. And until then, he wasn't going to give her a chance to jump ship before her explanations were deemed acceptable.

CARRIE GROANED and flung her arms out, pressing her palms into the mattress to steady the sway of the bed. For a long moment, she refused to open her eyes, certain that as soon as she did, her senses would be overwhelmed by the nausea. She felt sick, as if she had the flu or food poisoning. Or a really bad hangover—not that she'd ever had one. And then she remembered where she was.

"Oh, God," she cried. "I'm still on the damn boat."

"The question is, what are you *doing* on the damn boat?"

Startled by the unfamiliar voice, Carrie bolted upright. Her head snapped around, and her bleary eyes came to rest on a man lying next to her. She blinked and tried to focus. As soon as she did, the nausea doubled. Good Lord! Dev Riley was in her bed! And he was wearing nothing but silk boxers and a smile.

"I—I must be dreaming," she murmured, the room spinning around her, her mind whirling in the opposite direction. She rolled to her side and tried to convince herself that she was still asleep, pinching her eyes shut for good measure and taking a few deep breaths. "Oh, please. I have to be dreaming."

"This is no dream, sweetheart."

Sweetheart? Dev Riley was in her bed, in his underwear, and he was calling her "sweetheart?" Oh, this was definitely a dream. But her eyes wouldn't stay closed. And she could smell his cologne in the air, hear the water rushing against the hull of the boat. And this nausea! If this were really a dream, she would feel...well, she'd feel a lot better.

Slowly, Carrie pushed up to a sitting position and faced him at the very same moment that she faced her fears. *So let's say he is real,* she mused. What was he doing here? And how did they end up on the same—Susie! Susie had done this to her! Lured her down to Miami under false pretenses and tossed her into bed with Dev Riley.

"I'm not dreaming, am I," she murmured.

He grinned and shook his head, his gaze dropping to her chest.

Carrie groaned again, then glanced down to see the sheet revealing a little too much skin. With a tiny scream, she snatched the sheet up to her chin and wriggled to the edge of the bed, all the while keeping her eyes on him.

Susie had arranged the whole thing: the trip, the shared cabin, this forced intimacy with her fantasy man...although it was hard to believe Susie had arranged those silk boxers he wore. If Carrie didn't miss her guess, *Serendipity* was already underway, far enough from land to make a quick escape impossible. Susie had probably arranged for that, too!

"I think I'm going to throw up," she moaned, trying to struggle to her feet.

"Before you throw up, maybe you can tell me who you are. And what you're doing in my cabin."

Carrie swallowed. "I can't talk right now."

She heard him curse, and a few moments later he appeared beside her. "Here. Take this."

Her gaze drifted up his long, muscular legs to his boxers, then stopped in the vicinity of his lap, riveted to the faint outline of his... "Oh, my," she murmured.

Dev pushed the glass of water at her, and, with a trembling hand, she grabbed it along with the dose of medication, grateful for a momentary distraction. "Take it," he ordered. "Then we're going to talk."

Carrie did as she was told, trying to sort out her thoughts as she sipped the water. Susie had booked them on the same trip, in the same cabin. Yet Dev didn't know who she was. He didn't recognize her. So he couldn't possibly know this was Susie's idea of a setup. And what about his——? Carrie groaned again and buried her face in the twisted sheet. Had Susie found some way to get rid of his girlfriend as well? How could she possibly have arranged that?

Jillian—that was her name. His fiancée. Carrie moaned inwardly. Lying in bed next to him, naked, was humiliating enough. The only way matters could get any worse would be if his girlfriend walked in the door and caught them together. "Maybe if I just go back to sleep," Carrie said, rubbing her forehead. "This is all too confusing right now."

"Imagine how I felt when you curled up in my arms and kissed me," Dev said.

Carrie glanced up at him, her eyes wide. Kissed him? She'd kissed Dev Riley? How could she have missed such a momentous event? "You and I—" She drew a long breath. "We kissed...on the lips...in bed?"

His dark eyebrow quirked up, and he grinned one of those devastating grins that made her mind turn to mush. "On the lips," he confirmed. "In bed. It was very passionate. The earth moved, the angels sang."

Stunned, Carrie sat up and the sheet fell to her waist. With a soft cry, she snatched it up and tucked it under her arms. This was exactly why people shouldn't sleep naked! A person never knew who they might wake up with. "What else did I—I mean, we—do?"

Dev laughed. "You don't remember?" He clutched his hands to his naked chest. "I'm hurt. Usually, I'm very memorable. In fact, I'm so memorable that most women want to relive the moment—again and again and—"

"I get the picture," Carrie muttered, her heart banging against her chest. How could she have slept through it all? She'd made love to her perfect fantasy man, and she couldn't remember a single moment of the event. Unless... She glanced up at him again and caught a twinkle of amusement in his eyes. Could he be teasing her? Carrie cleared her throat and readjusted the sheet.

She couldn't just come out and call him a liar.

And a secret part of her wanted to think that the dream she'd had the previous night was real. Even if she didn't remember it, it had to have been one of the most exciting events of her life. Still, she would have remembered, wouldn't she? Carrie cleared her throat. "W-was I good?" she asked.

"Good? You were incredible. So passionate and uninhibited."

She ground her teeth. Fat chance! He was lying, making fun of her. And for that, she wanted to make him pay. She wanted to wipe that smug little smirk right off his handsome face. "That's amazing," she said in a soft voice, "considering it was my first time. I always dreamed it would be perfect." She frowned. "I also thought I'd remember it."

His grin froze and his green eyes widened. "Your first time? You mean you're a..." He let his voice drift off, and she could see regret in his expression. Now whose turn was it to smile smugly?

Carrie sighed dramatically. "Umm-hmm. The very first time I've ever—" she drew a deep breath and narrowed her eyes "—ever met such a black-hearted, despicable, conceited, lying sonofa—"

He held up his hand. "All right, all right. Your point is made," he interrupted. "There's no need to disparage my mother. And I'm sorry for embellishing the truth. But you have to understand my surprise at finding you in my bed."

Carrie struggled to her feet, keeping the sheet wrapped tightly around her. "I might not know exactly what happened here, but I do know that we didn't make love."

Dev opened his mouth, then snapped it shut.

"Well, we could have, if I hadn't been such a gentleman. And you hadn't been nearly comatose."

"And if I weren't a lady, I'd start screaming for the captain right about now."

"Hey, you're the one who's in *my* cabin." Dev backed away from the bed, then slouched down in a chair. "Why don't we start with your name?"

"It's Car—ah..." She bit back the rest, knowing that she shouldn't reveal her name. If he recognized it, then he might put two and two together and jump to the wrong conclusion: that *she* had deliberately planned this encounter just to get closer to him. But then, he'd always worked with Susie, and there was no reason for him to know Carrie's name. It wasn't painted on the front door or emblazoned across the company stationery.

"Cara? Cara what?"

"Carin," she quickly corrected. "Carin Reynolds." Such a boring name—not nearly as exotic and alluring as *Jillian.* "But my friends call me Carrie." *Cara* sounded much more sophisticated than *Carrie,* didn't it? *Carrie* sounded like a ninety-year-old maiden aunt. *Cara* sounded almost as good as *Jillian.*

She watched him carefully, waiting for some hint of recognition, but there was nothing. They'd come face-to-face on the street just a few mornings before, she owned the travel agency he visited at least twice a month—and he didn't have a clue! Carrie's heart twisted with indignation. So much for being memorable.

"And where are you from, Ms. Reynolds?"

She couldn't say Lake Grove, or even Chicago. Carrie searched her memory for an obscure spot on the globe, a place that Dev Riley couldn't possibly know intimately. "I'm from all over," she said. "My father was…a salesman. Mostly we lived in— in Anchorage. Alaska. Are you familiar with Anchorage?"

"I've been there a few times," he said.

"Well, we didn't live there long before we moved to Helena. Montana."

Dev shook his head. "I'm afraid I've never been to Helena."

Carrie breathed a silent sigh of relief. She knew all the places that Dev had visited—they were all on her computer. How had she missed Anchorage? So she'd be Carin Reynolds from Helena, Montana. As long as he didn't know her true identity, she could make her escape without being discovered. She could go back to Lake Grove and carry on as if she'd never agreed to this disastrous vacation. And when Dev Riley stepped inside her office again, he'd barely give her a second glance.

She twisted her fingers together in nervous knots. "Helena is the capital of Montana—did you know that? Although Great Falls should be, since it's more in the geographical center of the state. Montana is called The Treasure State. It's the fourth-largest state." Dev frowned at her as if she'd suddenly started speaking Greek. Carrie forced a smile and decided that it was a good time to stop babbling.

"Now that we've finished our little geography lesson," Dev said, "why don't you tell me what you're doing here?"

"Would you mind if we had this conversation

fully clothed?" Carrie asked, tugging the sheet up on her chest.

"And give up my advantage? As long as you're taking cover beneath the covers, you can't avoid my questions. How did you end up in this cabin?"

Carrie drew in a deep breath, then gave him an innocent shrug. "It was obviously a mistake. I thought my travel agent was sending me to a resort. With lots of rooms...and more than one bed."

"And I booked this charter for two. That's all this boat carries."

"So where's your traveling companion?" Carrie snapped. "She wasn't in bed with us, too, was she?"

His jaw went tight. "She canceled."

"Well, that's it, then. They double-booked the cabin. It happens all the time in the travel industry. Perhaps Captain Fergus thought you intended to cancel as well, and that's why he took my reservation."

"But he was expecting me and my companion. In fact, he thought *you* were my companion. How do you explain that?"

Carrie felt her temper rise. "If you're implying that I tricked my way on board then—"

His eyebrow shot up again. "Did you? There are plenty of women who'd love to find themselves in bed with Devlin Riley for more reasons than I'd care to count. Are you one of those women, Ms. Reynolds? If that's really your name."

Of all the arrogant, condescending males she'd ever met, Devlin Riley took first prize! Could he be so egotistical as to believe that women—no, that *she*—would deviously weasel her way into his bed? How could she have even imagined herself attracted to someone so smug and self-absorbed? Even worse, how could such a creep still cause her heart to pound and her head to spin?

Carrie wrapped the sheet more snugly around her, then stalked across the cabin to stand at the door. "Get out of my cabin, Mr. Riley."

"This is *my* cabin, Ms. Reynolds."

"I was here first, and possession is nine points of the law."

He pushed to his feet, crossed to the door and bent perilously close to her. "*Possession,*" he murmured. "That's a dangerous word to be tossing around when you've got nothing on but a bedsheet."

Carrie ground her teeth, then spun around and grabbed his trousers from the end of the bed. She threw them at his head, and yanked the cabin door open. "Get out."

With a charming grin, Dev tossed his pants over his shoulder and sauntered out the door, whistling as he walked. "We're not finished this conversation," he said from the companionway, his back to her.

Carrie punctuated the slam of the cabin door with a caustic oath. "How could I have been so stupid?" she muttered. "My fantasy man? This vacation is a nightmare, and he's the boogeyman!"

Dropping the sheet, she bent down to retrieve fresh clothes from her suitcases. She finally found a sundress that wasn't too wrinkled, and tugged it over her head. Her hair looked a mess, and she reached for her makeup bag, then scolded herself.

After he'd disparaged her character, how could she still care what Dev Riley thought about her?

How had she managed to build him into such a paragon of manhood? All her fantasies and daydreams were built on nothing but pure imagination. Still, he was handsome and charming and undeniably attractive—and just looking at him made her breathless....

Carrie groaned and yanked a brush through tangled hair. She should hate him, but all she could work up was a mild case of righteous indignation. After all, he was quite gallant that day on the icy sidewalk. And he *had* been a gentleman in bed, even when confronted with a warm and willing woman.

"Don't make excuses for him!" she muttered, tossing her brush on the bed. He was a scoundrel, a cad with an ego the size of Switzerland. Insinuating that she'd put herself in that bed to seduce him! How dare he?

In an attempt to calm her anger, Carrie sat down on the rumpled bed and weighed all her options. She'd have to get off this boat. The last thing she needed was for Dev Riley to find out how she ended up on his vacation and in his bed. Or to realize how infatuated she was with him, in spite of his boorish behavior.

"I don't know where we are, but we have to be close to land," she murmured aloud. Carrie reached for the door. She'd explain the error to Captain Fergus, and he'd turn the boat toward the nearest port. She'd ignore Dev Riley for the remainder of her time on board *Serendipity*. And if all went well, she'd be rid of her silly fantasies—and the man who had inspired them—by the time the sun set.

"THERE'S BEEN SOME MIX-UP," Dev explained.

Captain Fergus stood at the helm and stared out at the deep turquoise water, as Dev settled himself at a breakfast table set beneath a green-striped canopy. "Your accommodations aren't to your satisfaction?" the captain asked, squinting into the early morning sun. "If there's anything more you want, Moira will be happy to get it for you."

Dev savored a sip of freshly squeezed orange juice, then shook his head. "The accommodations are fine," he replied. "It's the woman sharing my cabin. She's a stranger."

A very entertaining stranger, Dev mused, but a stranger all the same. With a soft, lush body that she'd barely hidden beneath that bedsheet. All at once, she was sweet and vulnerable and stubborn and impertinent. A confusing mix of childish bravado and tantalizing allure. And she had a temper, too!

He'd come to the quick conclusion that her appearance in his cabin had been a simple mistake. She didn't seem the deceitful type. Still, he did find her piqued anger and stammered indignation amusing.

"A stranger, you say?" Captain Fergus chuckled. "Ah, lad. This happens all the time. The prospect of spending days in such close quarters. In my opinion, every couple should spend a week or two on a sailboat before they jump into marriage. It would certainly weed out the matrimonial weaklings."

Dev picked up his fork and cut into a thick omelette filled with peppers and cheese. "You don't understand. Until last night, I'd never seen that woman before."

"A lover's quarrel. A romantic lunch for two at a secluded beach on Elliott Key will put everything to rights. I'll have Moira start the preparations."

Dev ground his teeth. He sure hoped Captain Fergus wasn't as obtuse about navigational matters as he was about matters of the heart, or they'd end up in Ecuador. "I don't *know* the woman in my cabin. My companion, Jillian Morgan, canceled at the last minute. I came on this trip alone."

"Then Ms. Reynolds isn't your—"

"That's what I'm saying. She's a stranger. We hadn't met...until last night."

The captain shook his head and clucked his tongue. "It's those damn computers. I told Moira that you can't trust a machine to do a first mate's work. Another mix-up, I'm afraid."

"You mean this has happened before?"

"This is what we get for signing on to a computer reservations service. The wife thought it would cut down on the paperwork, but I thought—"

"The point is," Dev interrupted, "I paid for that cabin in full. And she doesn't belong there. You're going to have to find her another cabin."

Captain Fergus scratched his chin. "Well, now. There's the problem. You see, she paid for her passage in full, too. And we only have one other cabin—the one we store the luggage in. It's not nearly as luxurious—just a few hammocks and a porthole. We use it for the grandkids when they're on board. It's not fitted out for guests. I suppose you and—"

Their conversation was interrupted by a commotion coming from the forward cabin. A moment later, a suitcase appeared in the main hatchway, followed by another. Dev heard a soft curse before an overnight bag tumbled out onto the deck. Carrie Reynolds followed, stumbling over the suitcases scattered around her feet. When she glanced up and noticed them watching her, she blushed. Then just as quickly, she regained her composure, smoothing her skirt and running her fingers through her tousled hair.

Dev couldn't help but smile. She looked so mussed, so skittish, as if she'd simply fly apart at any minute. He held out a glass of juice. "Breakfast, Ms. Reynolds?"

She scowled at him, then turned her attention to the captain. "I want to get off this boat! I need to get off this boat. How far are we from land?"

The captain smiled apologetically. "I'm terribly sorry, Ms. Reynolds. Mr. Riley explained the problem."

"I'm sure he did," Carrie muttered, sending Dev a sideways glare. "So, we need to find land so I can get off this boat. I need an airport, any place that has a plane to fly me back to Miami. This is not the vacation I signed on for. There was supposed to be a resort with room service and massages and a swimming pool and a—" her face suddenly went white and she pressed her fingers to her lips "—a place where the floor doesn't pitch and roll and...oh, my."

"Maybe some toast would help?" Dev suggested.

Carrie wobbled toward the table, then gripped the edge with a white-knuckled hand. Her fingers trembling, she snatched the triangle of toast from him and took a bite. "How—how long until we reach land?"

"About three hours," Captain Fergus replied, glancing over his shoulder.

She pulled out the bench and sat down with a soft moan. "Three hours." Carrie drew a long, deep breath. "Three hours. If I just sit right here and concentrate, I can make it for another three hours."

Dev watched as she closed her eyes, but a few seconds later, her face went pale again and her eyelids fluttered open. He held out another piece of toast, and she grudgingly took it. "It's better to keep your eyes open and fixed on the horizon," he suggested. "Seasickness is all an inner ear, balance thing. If you can get your bearings, you'll feel much better."

"I don't need your advice," she muttered, munching on the toast.

"I'm just trying to be helpful," Dev said. She looked so utterly miserable that he felt compelled to do something for her. Though he'd never been overly protective toward women before, Carrie Reynolds just seemed to be the type that needed someone to watch out for her. After all, if he wasn't keeping an eye on her, she might trip and fall overboard, knock herself unconscious with her luggage or—

Dev bit back a chuckle. She surely wasn't the picture of feminine grace. But he found her clumsiness quite endearing. After all, not every woman in the world was cut out for climbing mountains or trekking across the desert. Sitting on a sailboat was just about her speed—if it weren't for the seasickness.

Besides, a real woman shouldn't look perfect every minute of the day and night. Carrie Reynolds was a regular woman, and she wasn't afraid to show it. He had to admire that about her.

Her hair fluttered against her face in the salty breeze, and he found his attention transfixed by a strand that caressed her pale neck. She watched the horizon, her profile outlined by the early morning sun. And then she turned…and caught him staring. For a moment, he thought she might smile. But then, she pressed her lips together and reached for her napkin. "Thank you," she said. "I do feel a little better."

"So would you like to try something else? This omelette is pretty good. And there's grilled ham."

A reluctant smile touched the corners of her mouth, and it warmed him as much as the tropical sun. "I am pretty hungry."

"Good," Dev said, cutting his omelette in half and placing it on her plate. "You'll feel much better after you eat."

Carrie dug into her breakfast with all the gusto of a starving sailor. He'd never seen anyone enjoy food quite as much as she did. Jillian ate like a bird and was always picking apart her meals, discarding anything that resembled a fat gram. But Carrie ate her half of the omelette along with what was left of his half, another piece of toast, two pieces of ham and half the pitcher of orange juice. By the time she finished, her color had returned and she looked almost content.

Dev leaned back in his chair and studied her. "Tell me about yourself, Carin Reynolds. Besides the fact that you enjoy a good breakfast."

"It's Carrie," she said. "Ms. Reynolds to you."

"All right, Carrie. Let's start with your personal life. Are you married? Engaged? Seriously involved?"

"That's none of your business."

"Ah, but it is. We spent the night together. I'm curious about the woman who warmed my bed."

"It was *my* bed," she countered. "I was there first. And—and we barely touched."

"All right. I'll concede those two points. As for the third, the touching part...well, you did touch me. There's no denying that."

A long silence descended over the breakfast table, the snapping of the sails the only sound. "There's not much to tell," she finally said, ignoring the bait. "I lead a pretty ordinary life."

"Yet here you are, taking an extraordinary vacation. Alone. This didn't come cheap. What do you do for a living?"

"This isn't the vacation I was supposed to have! My travel agent made a mistake. Once I get off this boat, I can have the vacation I paid for."

"You could stay if you wanted," Dev said.

She shook her head, more annoyed than surprised by his offer. "I'm sure some women would find that proposal irresistible, Mr. Riley—spending a few more days in your presence...in your bed. But—"

"I'm not suggesting we share a bed, Carrie. There is another cabin on board. It's not quite as nice, but—"

"No," Carrie said. "I appreciate your offer to move, but I—"

"*I'm* not offering to move," Dev said. "I meant that you could take the other cabin."

"B-but I was here first!" she sputtered.

"But your travel agent made the mistake, not mine. You said so yourself."

She crumpled up her napkin and tossed it on the table. "Whoever said chivalry was dead, was wrong. It's not just dead, it's buried under miles of the modern male ego." She pushed away and stood up, but she obviously hadn't completely gained her sealegs. Her knees buckled, and she reached for the table.

Dev stood and grabbed her by the shoulders before she lost her balance completely. "Hey! Are you all right?" He looked down into her wide eyes, and a wave of déjà vu washed over him. For an instant, he felt as if he knew her, and he swore he saw a flash of recognition in her gaze as well. But the feeling passed so quickly that he must have only imagined it.

"I'm fine," she said, twisting out of his grasp. "I just need to get off this boat."

"Maybe you should lie down. You can take the cabin—I don't care."

"No, I'll just stay outside." With that, she tiptoed through her luggage and found a spot on the forward deck. Gingerly, she sat down and turned her gaze toward the horizon.

Dev slouched back into his chair and wove his

fingers together behind his head. To be honest, he was hoping that she'd decide to stay. He could use the company, and Carrie Reynolds wasn't at all disagreeable as a traveling companion. She didn't seem too impressed by his charm though; in fact, she was downright prickly toward him.

Hell, what did he care what she thought of him? He'd come on this vacation to get away from women. If he had to spend his time with one, she might as well hate him. That way he'd be able to avoid any thought of how he was going to get Carrie Reynolds back into his bed.

nation.

3

THE SUN BEAT DOWN on the narrow road that ran
from the yacht club to the tiny airstrip. Carrie had
convinced Captain Fergus that it was imperative
that she get back to Miami, and he had bypassed
their stop on Elliott Key and navigated to the
northern end of Key Largo. She'd expected the
town from the Bogart movie—a civilized spot—
when she disembarked. But they were merely on
the same island as Key Largo, and nowhere close
to the real town that shared the island's name.

Key Largo was just a bump of land in the ocean,
a mile-wide sandbar with lush vegetation. Outside
the confines of the lavish yacht club, there was a
small residential area with lovely homes and a few
businesses. She'd managed to find a taxi, a battered
car that offered rides to wheel-less sailors. Carrie
had gratefully tossed her luggage in the trunk and
directed the driver to the airport.

The landscape that flew by was probably quite
lovely. But Carrie couldn't see much through the
cloud of dust kicked up by the battered taxi. "Airstrip's just down this road!" Her driver was just a
kid, barely old enough to see above the wheel. His
long hair whipped over his eyes, and he drove
with one hand, the other in constant use keeping
his vision clear. Music blared from the radio, so

loud she couldn't tell whether it was rap or Rachmaninoff.

Carrie moved to close the windows in the back, then realized the cab didn't have any windows. "I've died and gone to vacation hell," she murmured, coughing and waving her hand in front of her face.

She'd gotten off the boat as soon as it docked, scrambling onto the wooden pier, grateful to put solid, unmoving ground beneath her feet. Captain Fergus and his wife Moira continued to offer profuse apologies, but no amount of convincing would get her back on *Serendipity*. Dev Riley had watched her the whole time, his shoulder braced against the mast, his arms crossed over his bare chest.

If she'd still been a woman prone to fantasy, Carrie might have imagined that he was sorry to see her go. She might have dreamed that the firm set of his jaw, his implacable expression, his emotionless green eyes, merely hid his true feelings. But she knew better now.

That was the problem with fantasies. They faded quickly in the harsh light of reality. She'd built Dev Riley into some image of masculine perfection. And though, outwardly, the fantasy held up, she'd been forced to admit that the man was more than a gorgeous face and hard, muscular body. He was stubborn and opinionated and irritating.

The taxi careened around a curve, the back end fishtailing and tossing her to one side. She gripped the armrest and gritted her teeth. If she could just hold on for a few more hours, she'd be all right. She could settle into a nice hotel in Miami, she could get a good night's sleep, and then tomorrow, she could go home and forget this nightmare had ever happened.

An image of Dev Riley flashed in her mind— shirtless, his long, muscular legs and arms burnished by the sun. Had she been braver, more confident, she might have stayed. A week alone with a man like Dev would have been a dream come true. But after just one morning with him, she was honest enough to admit that he was well out of her league. Witty repartee was not her strong suit, and Dev seemed to thrive on sparkling conversation and sly innuendo. He'd bait and tease her, then sit back and wait for her to rise to the challenge.

When she got back home, she'd forget all about him. And when he came into the agency, she'd barely take notice. He'd be like any other client. Just another guy in a cashmere overcoat...with gorgeous green eyes...and the profile of a Greek god.

"Here we are!" the cabdriver called. The cab skidded to a halt at the end of a narrow clearing, and Carrie hopped out. "That's my uncle's plane over there. He's usually not too far away."

Her luggage thudded to the ground, raising another small cloud of dust, and Carrie squinted as she pulled her wallet from her purse and paid the cabbie. "When is the next flight out?" Carrie asked.

The cabbie pointed toward the lone plane. "Whenever Pete takes off."

"There must be more than one airline here."

The kid shook his head. "Sometimes, if there's more than one plane parked here. But don't worry, Pete'll fly you anywhere for the right price."

"Fine," Carrie said, grabbing her suitcase and gathering her resolve. "I'm just going to go over there and buy my ticket." *And get off this godforsaken sand dune*, she added silently.

Carrie glanced around at the grass runway cut from the thick vegetation, and the tin shack that sat on one end. A wind sock with a hole in the toe was the only sign that this was a real airport. Except for that, the airstrip looked more like a farmer's field carved out of the dense underbrush.

She started across the scruffy tarmac, dragging her suitcases behind her, the wheels bumping along the hard ground. By the time she reached the plane, she was sweaty and dirty and out of breath—and close enough to get a good look at the transportation she'd chosen to take over a major body of water. The plane looked as if it was held together with chewing gum and duct tape. Dents and scratches marred the rusty fuselage, and one of the tires was noticeably flat.

A quiet mutter, the words indistinguishable, came from the other side of the plane. She bent down and saw a pair of battered sandals and saggy socks. "Excuse me!" she called.

"Third tee. Pebble Beach," was the only reply.

"I'm looking for a ride back to the mainland," Carrie said, circling the plane. "The kid who runs the taxi service said you can fly me back to Miami."

As she caught sight of the pilot, Carrie stopped in her tracks. The man, dressed in a loud Hawaiian shirt, paid no attention to her. Instead, he rolled a golf ball out in front of him, eyed it for a few seconds as he chewed on his cigar, swung his club back, then launched the ball down the length of the runway with a loud *thwack*. Each shot was followed by a muttered commentary.

His face, like those of many of the locals she'd seen, was weathered by the harsh Florida sun, permanent squint lines bracketing his eyes. The only thing that kept him from looking completely disreputable was the gray that peppered the closely cropped hair visible under his baseball cap. That and the gold wings that he had pinned crookedly to his shirt.

"Are you the pilot?" Carrie asked.

"Lieutenant Colonel Pete Beck. U.S. Navy. Retired." He studied another golf ball. "Seventeenth tee. Augusta." *Thwack*. He pointed to the ball. "Two hundred fifty-seven yards. Slight draw." He glanced back at her, carefully taking in her luggage. "There are other pilots roundabout this end of Key Largo. But I'm the only one here right now." *Thwack*. "This here plane is all mine. Bought and paid for."

Carrie looked at the plane again. She really longed to go to the Delta counter and buy a first-class ticket back home on a gleaming jet plane. She wanted pretty flight attendants and rubbery chicken, a little bag of peanuts and a seat cushion that could be used as a flotation device. But Lieutenant Pete was the only way back to Miami, short of getting back on another boat, or sticking out her thumb on the highway.

Carrie had already been through hell on this vacation. Hopping on a plane with a golf-obsessed aviator was infinitely preferable to another bout of seasickness—or facing Dev Riley at every turn. "Can you to fly me back to Miami?"

"I can fly you anywhere, if you've got the cash."

"How much?" she asked, mentally counting the money she had left in her wallet. Pete didn't look like the type to take American Express.

The pilot rubbed his whiskered chin, then gave her the once-over, silently calculating the depth of her wallet and her determination to leave the island. "Four hundred," he said.

Carrie gasped. "Four-hundred dollars? For a thirty-minute flight, one way? Florida Air runs a flight from Key West to Miami, and that's twice as far, for only $150.00. Round trip."

Pete chuckled. "Well, I'm not Florida Air, missy. And we're not in Key West, are we? And I just happen to need four hundred to buy my way on to eighteen holes at a pretty little country club in West Palm Beach. Take it or leave it."

Her temper snapped, hastened by the oppressive heat of the midday sun and the bead of sweat that trickled down her back. Carrie let go of her luggage and grabbed the man by his shirt. "Listen, mister," she said, trying to keep the hysterical tone from her voice. "I need to get off this island, and you're the only way off. You're going to fly me to Miami for a reasonable price, or I'm going to have a nervous breakdown right here on your damn runway. Do we have an understanding?"

For a moment, she thought he might relent, but then he set his jaw and narrowed his eyes. It was clear that she'd underestimated the pilot's tolerance for feminine hysteria. "Three hundred," he growled. "Cash. That's as low as I'll go."

With that, he turned back to his golf club, whacking another round of balls to the end of the runway. Carrie surveyed the plane, then the pilot, weighing her options. She had three-hundred dollars in her wallet, but her practical nature just wouldn't allow her to pay more for a flight than it was worth! And Carrie Reynolds knew better than any travel agent alive the precise value of travel between any two points on the planet.

For three-hundred dollars, she would spend another day with Dev Riley. Besides, upon further consideration, that choice was beginning to look like the lesser of two evils. At least she wouldn't crash and burn somewhere in the ocean with a pilot who was more concerned with his golf game than with the condition of his plane.

But then, she would make an idiot of herself with Dev, which would be much more painful than tumbling headlong into the ocean in a raging ball of fire. Carrie swallowed hard. "Three-hundred dollars is too much," she finally said, hoping he'd be willing to deal.

"Suit yourself," he replied with a shrug.

Carrie sighed, finally willing to admit defeat. "Well, then. I'll just be going back to the yacht club. My boat is waiting there. If I can use your phone to call the cab, I'd—"

"Can't call a cab," Lieutenant Pete said.

"You're not going to let me use your phone?"

He grinned. "I would if I had one—seein' as you're messin' with my concentration and gettin' on my nerves."

"Then how am I supposed to get back?"

"Suppose you'll have to walk."

"How do *you* get back to town?" Carrie asked.

He shrugged. "My nephew comes by every now and then, and I hitch a ride with him."

"When will he be back?"

The pilot shrugged again, a gesture that was starting to get on *her* nerves. "No tellin'. I 'spect if you need to get back to town, you might want to start walkin'. It's only about a mile, and it gets mighty hot in the afternoon."

With a vivid oath, Carrie picked up her luggage and did her best to turn smartly on her heel and stride away. "This is not happening to me," she muttered. "I haven't really slipped into some alternative dimension where vacation is a form of torture. I'm just having a...bad day. A *really* bad day."

As she trudged down the middle of the road, she silently chastised herself for losing her temper. Had she been more charming, she might have been able to come to a deal with Lieutenant Pete. He couldn't be completely immune to feminine wiles, could he? But she was tired and dirty and just a little crabby. And the man was gouging her on airfare!

By the time she reached the main road back to the yacht club, her arms felt at least five inches longer. Her cotton sundress clung to her body, and a thin film of dust covered every inch of exposed skin. She'd walked three-hundred yards and was exhausted from the effort of dragging her body weight in baggage. But she knew that if she ditched her bags, she might never see them again.

She'd managed another hundred yards when the sound of an approaching truck stopped her dead in the middle of the road. With a joyous cry, she turned and waved to the driver, hoping against hope he'd stop before he flattened both her and her luggage. When he did stop, Carrie ran up to the driver's side and put on her most grateful tourist smile. This time, she'd put a little charm to work for her.

The man in the truck could have passed for Lieutenant Pete's brother, except that he wore a battered straw hat instead of an old baseball cap. A cloud of smoke surrounded his head, emanating from the cigar that he had clenched between his teeth. "Yer in my way," he growled.

"I need to get back to the yacht club. Can you give me a ride?"

The man gave her the once-over, then shook his head. "Got to take these chickens out to the airstrip. Air freight's pickin' the lot up in twenty minutes."

"I'll pay you if you turn around. Fifty dollars. Cash."

He scowled, and she thought he'd refuse. "Hop in the back," he finally said.

Carrie frowned. There was no back seat to the truck. And a huge dog occupied the passenger side in the front. It was then she realized that she'd be expected to ride in the pickup bed. "Beggars can't be choosers," she murmured, hefting her luggage over the side. Her overnight bag jostled a small crate, and as she climbed in after it, a pair of chickens voiced their disapproval with a great screeching and flapping of wings.

The entire pickup was stacked with chicken crates, all of them at maximum occupancy. The smell nearly knocked her over, and at any moment, Carrie was certain that a chicken would break loose and attack her. As it was, chicken feathers filled the air, sticking to her damp skin and tangling in her hair as the pickup gained speed.

The road was rougher than she remembered it, and she spent most of the ride frantically trying to keep the crates from tumbling. By the time they reached the yacht club, she'd taken on the distinct odor of her traveling companions. The truck skidded to a stop and, as if she hadn't been humiliated enough in one day, a crate came crashing down on top of her. Several well-dressed yachtsmen and their ladies gaped at her as she crawled out of the back of the pickup.

Considering her luck, Carrie expected *Serendipity* to be gone from its spot at the dock. But the boat was still there, rocking gently against the pier, its wooden decks gleaming in the sun. She grabbed her bags from the truck, then hurried up to the driver's door, determined to thank her savior. Carrie dug in her purse for a fifty-dollar bill, then shoved it through the window, but the only reply she got was a grunt and a squeal of tires, accompanied by more dust and chicken feathers.

Carrie didn't plan to be quite so happy to step back on *Serendipity*, but she was. Too exhausted to bring her luggage back on board, she left it on the dock for Captain Fergus to haul over the rail. A quick search of the deck revealed that Fergus and first-mate Moira were nowhere to be found. Nor was Dev Riley.

She went below and found the main saloon empty. With a sigh of relief, Carrie slowly made her way forward, then flopped down on the soft bed that she'd slept on the night before, brushing a chicken feather from her nose. She closed her eyes and smiled, her battered body finally finding a bit of comfort.

So what if she was in Dev Riley's bed again! He wasn't around, and she just needed a few moments to regroup. Then she'd find that taxi driver and have him take her to the nearest bus station. Or maybe, for a decent price, he'd drive her all the way back to Miami. But for now, nothing short of a nuclear detonation would get her off this bed. And as for Dev Riley, she'd deal with him later.

DEV STROLLED BACK to *Serendipity* along the waterfront, watching powerboats and sailboats as they headed out through the marked channel and into the ocean. The late afternoon sun was low in the sky, glittering across the turquoise-blue water.

After Carrie had made her abrupt departure, Fergus had suggested a trip to the crocodile refuge. Dev had caught one of the area's few taxis at the entrance to the yacht club and taken a quick ride out there. Though the refuge was closed to visitors, Dev could still watch the reptiles sunning themselves from a spot on the road, through a pair of binoculars provided by the driver. The young man informed him that the refuge sheltered about four hundred of the sharp-toothed beasts. He also told Dev to stay near the taxi, for there were rattlesnakes populating the ditches on either side of the road.

Dev had found the first sight-seeing trip of his vacation quite interesting, but not nearly as interesting as the conversation he'd had with the driver on the way back to the yacht club. The young man babbled on about a lady he'd taken out to the airstrip just before Dev's fare. This pretty young woman was so desperate to get back to Miami that she risked getting on a plane with the most notorious pilot in the Keys.

The driver found the entire incident quite amusing, then regaled Dev with stories about his uncle's exploits in the air. By the time the taxi reached the entrance to the yacht club, Dev had begun to feel guilty about sending Carrie Reynolds into the hands of such a disreputable man. But then, Carrie was an adult and she could make her own decisions. Besides, she was the one who wanted to leave. He really hadn't pushed her off the boat.

But then, he had teased and taunted her until she'd really had no choice in the matter. He should have seen how sensitive she was, and employed a more delicate approach in dealing with her. In all honesty, he'd taken out some of his anger toward Jillian on Carrie—something she really didn't deserve. After all, she was just looking for a comfortable place to sleep.

There was no use regretting his actions now. She was gone—probably back in Miami by now. He'd never see her again. Dev stared at the docks and caught sight of the flag that fluttered from the stern of *Serendipity*. He was alone now, yet somehow it didn't make him as happy as he had anticipated.

Rather than go back to the quiet solitude of the boat, Dev stopped at the yacht club's bar and restaurant and ordered one of the local specialties. The waitress brought him a cold beer along with a tasty dinner of fresh conch fritters. The patrons at the restaurant were a mix of bluewater sailors and locals, a colorful bunch that invited him into their conversations.

He shared a few more beers and a lively game of darts before he begged off and headed back to the boat. The sun had dropped below the horizon, and he waved at Captain Fergus as he approached, watching the man carefully fold a sail and stuff it into a bag.

His mind returned to Carrie Reynolds, and he realized that he'd half expected her to be on board when he got back. Though they'd only spent one night together—chaste by his standards—he couldn't help but feel a connection to her. She'd been so different, so intriguing. So damn difficult. Carrie Reynolds hadn't been his type, but she did possess a certain goofy charm that he found attractive. And she hadn't been hard to look at. In truth, she had been quite pretty, even to his jaded eye. He'd almost welcome another battle over the berth, but he'd have his bed all to himself tonight.

He kicked off his boat shoes and stepped on board. Captain Fergus called out to him, asking if he wanted dinner, but Dev waved him off. The conch fritters and the beer had been plenty. As he crossed to the hatch, he tugged his T-shirt over his head before stepping down into the cabin.

As his eyes adjusted to the dim light, he gasped in surprise. The main saloon was littered with his clothes. Shorts and shirts lay scattered around his overturned luggage. Towels from the shower she'd obviously taken strewn over chairs. With a soft curse, he crossed the saloon and shoved open the door to his berth.

She was curled up on the bed, a pillow clutched

to her chest, and her mussed hair covering her eyes. For a moment, he thought she might be asleep, but then he heard a soft sniffle. "You're back," he said.

"You're observant," she replied.

"I suspected as much when I noticed someone had tossed all my stuff out of here," he said dryly. "I also noticed you're in my bed."

Carrie threw her arm over her face and groaned. "It's my bed now and I'm not leaving. Just go away. I want to be alone."

Dev closed the door behind him and leaned against it. He brushed aside an unbidden feeling of delight at seeing her. She'd decided to leave, and now she was back. He shouldn't have missed her, but he did, and that realization made him a little annoyed. He usually had such tight control over his feelings, but when it came to Carrie Reynolds, all his control seemed to vanish.

Now, looking at her in his bed, all he could think about was joining her there. He fought the urge to lie down beside her, pull her into his arms and kiss her long and hard. The taste of her lips was still fresh in his mind, and he craved that taste now. Dev drew a slow, deep breath. "I thought you wanted to get back to Miami."

"We don't always get what we want."

"I always get what I want," Dev said, his tone even.

"Just try to throw me out," she muttered, her voice muffled by the pillow. "I dare you!"

Dev crossed his arms over his chest. "Now there's an interesting suggestion," he teased. "I might enjoy tossing you overboard."

She pushed up in bed; her hair tumbled over her face. "Leave me alone. I'm tired and dirty, and I smell like chickens. I've got a sunburn and a headache and you're getting on my nerves. This is as much my bed as it is yours, and I'm taking a nap now."

He sniffed, then wrinkled his nose. "Chickens? Is that what that smell is? Chickens?"

She shoved her hair out of her eyes and glared at him. "I'm going to stay on the boat until we get to a bigger town—someplace with a real airport and real planes, and then I'll leave. But until then, this is my bed. Got it?"

"And where am I supposed to sleep?"

"You can lash yourself to the mast for all I care."

Dev frowned and then bent lower to peer into her face. "Are you all right?"

She threw the pillow at his head. "I told you, I'm tired and I'm sunburned and I—"

"Have spots," Dev said, pointing to her cheeks, a grin quirking the corners of his mouth.

Her fingers flew to her face. "Spots? What kind of spots?"

Dev shook his head and approached the bed. He sat down on the edge and hooked his thumb beneath her chin, tipping her face up to the light from the starboard portholes. "Looks like measles. Or chicken pox. Only bigger. And redder. Did something bite you?"

With a strangled cry, Carrie scrambled out of bed, crawling over him to grab a small mirror from her purse. She flipped it open and squinted at her reflection. "Oh—oh, my. I have…dots. Polka dots. All over my face. You can't get chicken pox from chickens, can you? No, that's not possible. Besides, I've already had chicken pox."

She looked over at him, and he could swear she'd turned a deeper shade of pink—if that was possible. He'd never seen a woman who looked more pitiful than Carrie Reynolds did right now. Dev stretched out on the bed and linked his hands behind his head. Even with the spots, she still had the audacity to look beautiful, too. Try as he might, he couldn't take his eyes off her.

But Carrie didn't appreciate his intent stare. A tear popped from the corner of each eye right before she buried her sunburned face in her hands. Though he knew he should comfort her, his first thought was of escape. He'd never been able to handle a woman's tears—not that he'd had much experience.

With a hesitant step, he rolled off the berth and stood in front of her. Her shoulders shook with her weeping, and he winced, then cursed silently. "It's not that bad," he said. "With a little bit of makeup—some of that powder stuff you women wear—you won't even be able to tell. And it's not like it's permanent. The spots will go away." He paused. "Won't they?"

His words didn't seem to have any impact. She continued to tremble, her weeping muffled by her hands. Gently, he reached out and pried her fingers from her eyes. Her fingertips were wet with tears, and her blue eyes were watery with those still unshed. "It looks like a reaction to the sun," he said softly. "Sun poisoning."

"I don't know whatever possessed me to agree to this vacation. I shouldn't have come! I should have stayed home, where I don't feel like throwing up every second of the day. Where the sun stays behind the clouds and where I don't have to worry about—about spots!"

"Don't cry," he murmured, his gaze fixed on hers. "It's really not that bad."

"You're just saying that."

Dev grinned ruefully. "Yeah, I am just saying that. Right now, I'd say just about anything to get you to stop crying."

She sniffled, then managed a wavering smile. "Well, thank you, for trying to make me feel better."

Dev wasn't sure what possessed him at that instant. Whether it was her watery blue eyes, wide with expectation. Or her damp mouth, soft and inviting. All he could think about was the kiss they had shared in their bed the night before; the heat and the passion that had bubbled in his bloodstream. He wanted to feel that way again, to taste her sweet mouth and pull her lush body against his. And to have her respond to *him*, and not some dreamy image floating through her slumber.

The moment he bent closer and touched her lips, he was lost. His mind shut down, focusing entirely on the kiss. He expected resistance, but he encountered acceptance. Afraid to touch her, afraid to break the spell that had come over them both, he probed gently with his tongue. He groaned softly when she opened beneath him.

But when he grasped her shoulders, she drew back with a soft oath. He looked down to see pain in her eyes, and for a moment he thought she regretted what had just passed. Then he realized that she was in genuine pain—from her sunburned skin.

"I'm sorry," Dev said, backing away and holding his hands out.

She blinked, then frowned. "Sorry?"

His palms hovered over her shoulders, feeling the heat radiating from her skin. "You're in the tropics," Dev said softly. "Didn't you think to bring sunscreen?"

"Sure I did. I—I just didn't put it on. I just wanted to go home. That's all I was thinking of. And then the taxi drove off and left me at the airstrip with that awful pilot and his awful plane. And there were no phones. I had to walk to the main road and it was hot and—"

"You're not much of a traveler, are you?"

She frowned, oddly insulted by such an obvious observation. "I travel," Carrie said, a tinge of defensiveness creeping into her voice. "I've been all over the world. I—I was simply distracted."

Dev clasped his hands in front of him. "That's probably my fault. I feel partially responsible. After all, I'm the one who ruined your vacation."

"Thank you. I'm glad you've finally admitted that. This has been all your fault."

He grinned, then tweaked her red nose. "That still doesn't mean I'm going to give you my bed. For all I know, you got a sunburn on purpose just so I'd feel sorry for you."

With a scream of frustration, Carrie grabbed a pillow from the bed and swung it at him. He dodged it, then laughed. "A little too close to the truth?"

She cursed beneath her breath, then began to

gather her things from the cabin in a fit of temper. "I should have known you couldn't be nice for too long."

Dev smiled apologetically. "Carrie, I was teasing."

"Well, now you won't have anyone to tease. You can have the damn bed. Sleep well. I hope all your dreams are nightmares."

Regret raced through him. He should have sensed that she was teetering on the edge of hysterics. She'd probably been through hell that afternoon, trying to find a way off the island. She was sunburned and exhausted. Just a few minutes ago, she'd been in tears. Dev couldn't begin to fathom the ups and downs of a woman's emotional state, but he knew that he'd pushed her too far. "Carrie, I—"

"I'm leaving," she muttered. "I don't know how I could ever have liked you. You are such a—a jerk." With that, she was out the door, leaving him standing in the middle of the cabin, utterly baffled.

"You are smooth, Dev," he murmured. "A real prince. Just kiss her and then insult her. The perfect way to make friends and influence people. And a great strategy to get a woman into your bed."

Why couldn't he just put Carrie Reynolds out of his head? Why was he so preoccupied with touching her and kissing her? Dev cursed inwardly. So much for putting women out of his life. That little resolution had lasted about as long as his solitary afternoon watching crocodiles. Well, he was not about to be drawn into another romantic relationship. Not now, not ever—and certainly not with Carrie Reynolds.

After the sting of Jillian's desertion, maybe he was simply using Carrie to soothe his bruised ego. It would be obvious to even the most casual observer that she wasn't his type. Jillian had been so self-assured, so ambitious and assertive. Carrie Reynolds was her polar opposite: nervous and needy and a little naive. Still, she was beautiful. And sexy as hell.

"Watch yourself, Riley," he muttered. "You certainly don't need a woman who needs you more than you need her."

CARRIE SHOULD HAVE KNOWN her vacation wouldn't be all smooth sailing. But she never expected to be caught in the midst of a hurricane of emotion and confusion. With every passing minute, she came to regret her decision at the airstrip. Why hadn't she spent the money to get back to the mainland? In some secret corner of her heart had she wanted to stay with Dev?

One moment, he seemed like the perfect gentleman. And the next moment, he was pricking her temper and driving her crazy with his arrogance. She didn't want to be attracted to him, but she couldn't help herself. She loved the way he laughed and the way he moved. She could spend hours fantasizing about the feel of his hair between her fingers, or the way his skin would feel against her—

With a soft cry, she braced her arms and legs against the edges of the couch and tried to anticipate the pitch and roll of the boat. Somewhere over the past hour, they'd hit rough seas. For the fourth time that night, she rolled off her makeshift bed in the main saloon and hit the floor with a thud. She silently cursed Dev, then Captain Fergus, then the entire Atlantic Ocean.

Dev was probably lying in the middle of his comfortable bed at this very minute, chuckling over her predicament. But she wasn't about to admit defeat. She'd make him regret his teasing accusations—or she'd die trying.

Carrie sighed. All of this was so unnecessary. After all, he had been teasing. But any suggestion that she might be manipulating him rubbed her the wrong way. Her temper, combined with the sunburn and the lingering effects of his kiss, had caused her to lose all common sense and storm out, leaving him with the comfortable bed. Had she been in a joking mood, she might be sleeping on a soft mattress this very minute, and *he* might be trying to keep himself off the floor.

Cursing quietly, Carrie sat up and tossed aside her blanket. If she didn't find a way to stay in bed, she'd never get any sleep. And she'd have pretty purple bruises to complement her sunspots in the morning.

"I should just sleep on the floor," she muttered. She stood up, then nearly fell down again as the boat pitched on a wave. Maybe she could try one of the hammocks strung in the small cabin across from the bathroom. At least she couldn't fall out of a hammock, could she?

She made her way forward, bracing her feet and hands where she could to keep from toppling over. At least she hadn't felt a twinge of seasickness all night. One bright spot in the midst of so many disasters.

Carrie opened the door to the tiny sleeping berth. It was little more than a closet with two hammocks strung from side to side. She frowned as she stepped up to the mass of loose rope netting, wondering how a person got into such an odd accommodation. She attempted to sit in it first, but ended up going over backward, her feet flying over her head. Then she tried to throw her knee over it and slide into the hammock. When that didn't work, she straddled the hammock, then slowly balanced against the rocking as she lay down.

Obviously, a hammock would not be a sailor's first choice for sleeping. Her feet were higher than her head, and her body was folded at a sharp angle. The rope rubbed at her sunburned arms, and she winced every time she tried to adjust herself.

Once she got settled, she took a long breath and closed her eyes, determined to get some sleep. But with each movement of the waves, the hammock swayed. An ever-increasing nausea clutched at her stomach, and she swallowed hard. Admitting defeat, she tumbled from the hammock after only five minutes.

"This is ridiculous," Carrie muttered. "I have every right to sleep in a real bed!"

With that, she grabbed her blanket and headed for the forward cabin. Carrie raised her hand to rap on the door, before deciding that arrogance was more important that etiquette. She turned the knob and stepped inside. Dev looked up at her from the bed where he'd been reading a magazine. He wore a pair of wire-rimmed glasses, and he stared quizzically at her over the rims. He didn't say anything; in truth, he didn't even look surprised.

"I'm reclaiming my half of the bed," Carrie said as she crossed the room.

A smile quirked the corners of his mouth, but he still didn't say anything. Instead, he reached across the bed and drew the covers down on her side—an obvious invitation. She felt her temper rise. Just because she was coming back to his bed didn't mean that he could take liberties!

Carrie grabbed the two cushions from the armchairs in the cabin, then pulled the covers back up, tucking them neatly under the mattress. She placed the cushions at the center of the bed, then bolstered them with a pair of pillows from her side of the bed, creating a sturdy barrier. "We're merely sleeping in the same room," she said. "As long as you stay on your side and I stay on mine, we shouldn't have any problems."

"I don't know," Dev said. "I toss and turn a lot in my sleep. There's no telling what I might do."

Carrie flipped her blanket out and then pulled it up to her chin. "It's late. I'd like to go to sleep now, if you don't mind."

Dev chuckled softly, then reached over to put out the light on his side of the berth. But Carrie didn't feel comfortable in the dark. She quickly turned on the lamp on her side of the bed.

"I can't sleep with the light on," Dev said.

"And I won't sleep with it off," Carrie replied.

Dev pushed up and rolled over the barrier as if it weren't there. His body lay across hers, and she could feel the warmth of his skin through the cotton pajamas she wore. He flipped the light off, but didn't make a move to return to his side of the bed.

She couldn't see him in the pitch-black of the

cabin, but she could feel the soft caress of his breath on her lips. He was near, his body heavy on hers. Holding her breath, she waited, wondering if he planned to kiss her. If he did, she wouldn't refuse him. She craved that flood of desire that raced through her when their mouths touched.

"Sweet dreams, Carrie," he whispered, his voice coming out of the darkness.

Then he was gone, the delicious warmth disappearing, until she was left cold and alone on her side of the bed. Carrie drew a shaky breath and tried to banish the tingling warmth that raced through her limbs and pooled at her core. This was typical of her luck on this vacation. The first night she'd spent with Dev Riley, she'd slept through his kisses. And now, she'd lie awake wanting what she'd missed that first night.

She listened until his breathing grew slow and even. And then she turned to him and tried to make out his face in the dark. A feeble illumination from the boat's running lights filtered through the portholes, and she could almost see him.

Slowly, she reached out and touched his hair with her fingers, then drew her hand back. She'd spent such a long time fantasizing about this man. But now, even with all the troubles between them, she'd come to desire the reality much more than the fantasy.

4

CARRIE WASN'T SURE how long she slept, but the cabin was bright with the morning sun when she awoke. She held her breath and slowly worked her fingers out to touch the barrier she'd erected. But there was nothing on the other side except empty mattress and tangled sheets. She breathed a long sigh of relief and sat up.

She couldn't believe she'd spent another night in the same bed with Dev Riley! Fate had them crawling between the sheets for bizarre reasons. The first night—a mistake. The second night—necessity. Would there be a third night and a fourth? And what might transpire if there was?

A hazy fantasy drifted through her mind, and she closed her eyes and savored it for a moment. Though he could be an arrogant jerk at times, there was no doubt in her mind that he'd be a wonderful lover—strong and assured...masterful. She'd had lovers in the past, but sex had always frightened her a bit. She'd never known a man who could make her blood run hot and her body tremble in anticipation just at the mere thought of what might be.

That's what it should be like, Carrie mused, flopping back on the pillows. Heat and delirious need. Overwhelming passion. A frantic climb toward a shattering climax…and then perfect satisfaction. A sigh slipped from her lips. At least, that's what she'd read in all those magazine articles. Proper lovemaking required tossing aside all inhibitions. With Dev, she just might be able to do that.

After all, she had walked right into this very cabin last night and crawled into bed with him. The Carrie Reynolds she'd always known would never do something so bold and impulsive. But Carrie Reynolds, intrepid vacationer, bluewater sailor, and aspiring femme fatale was different. A little adventure had an intoxicating effect on her confidence.

A soft knock sounded on the door, and she pushed up, reining in her fantasy and wincing at the pain in her sunburned arms and shoulders. If she really wanted Dev, then why not make her feelings more apparent? She could be alluring and tantalizing—if she put her mind to it. Carrie tugged her baggy pajama top off one shoulder, revealing just a little more skin. Then she ran her fingers through her tangled hair and took a deep breath. "Who is it?" she called, expecting Dev to answer.

"It's Moira, dear. May I come in?"

Before Carrie could contain her disappointment, Moira had already stepped through the door, a tray balanced on her hip and a shopping bag hooked over her arm. "I brought you some breakfast," she said. "Mr. Riley said you might want to sleep late." Moira gave her a knowing look. "I hear you didn't get much sleep last night."

Carrie gasped. "He said that? Well, I can assure you that nothing happened here. We slept together, but we didn't *sleep* together. It was like...camping." She smoothed the sheets, then folded her hands in front of her.

"I'm sure it was. But I believe he was referring to your sunburn, dear," Moira said, her round face and sweet smile exuding motherly sympathy. "He said you were a bit uncomfortable and restless." She set the tray on the bed and held up a tube of ointment. "He had us radio to a doctor in Key Largo for this last night. It'll help those little spots on your face."

Her fingers flew to her cheeks. She'd forgotten the spots! Oh, how humiliating—trying to be sexy when she looked like a kid with chicken pox. It was lucky Dev hadn't been at the door. It would have been just another opportunity to make a fool of herself. "He sent for this?" she asked.

Moira took the tube and squeezed a bit on her finger, then gently applied it to Carrie's face. The ointment immediately salved the burn, cooling her skin to a tolerable temperature. "Then he hired a driver to bring it down to Tavernier, then a boat to deliver it out here this morning. I'd wager he paid a pretty price for that delivery. He also got you a few other comforts, dear. Some pretty creams and lotions, bath oil and a lovely nightdress made of the softest fabric."

"Dev Riley did that for me?" Carrie grabbed the bag and carefully examined the contents, baffled by his unexpected generosity. If he were willing to pay for these comforts, why was he so stingy about sharing his bed?

"He's quite worried about you, dear. I'd guess he's feeling a wee bit guilty over your little tiff. I'm so glad you two worked out your problems. You're a lovely couple."

Carrie groaned. "We don't have problems, Moira. We're not a couple. We don't even know each other. We're strangers."

"Strangers sleeping in the same bed," Moira countered, refusing to accept the truth. "Well, that boy has a fine way of treating strangers, I'd say."

"As soon as I can find a way back to Miami, I'm leaving," Carrie murmured.

With a long sigh, Moira stood and clasped her hands together. "I'd better be tidying up now. We've dropped anchor, and if you'd like to take a trip into town after lunch, we'd be happy to show you about. You can find that way back to Miami, if you're that set on leaving. You just let us know when you're ready."

She slipped out of the cabin, leaving Carrie to a delicious meal of crispy French toast and sausage. After she finished breakfast, she slathered her body with the creams Dev had bought her. Then she slipped into a loose and comfortable sundress and tugged a wide-brimmed sunhat on her head. She almost felt normal, well rested and...happy. And though she didn't want to admit it, she was anxious to find Dev and thank him for his thoughtfulness.

The balmy ocean breeze cooled her skin the moment she stepped into the forward cockpit. She waved at Captain Fergus, who stood in the aft cockpit, bent over his charts. Carrie looked up and her breath caught in her throat. They were moored in the most beautiful spot she'd ever seen: a tiny cove surrounded by a white sand beach. Mangroves ringed the beach and rustled in the wind and the water was so blue that it hurt her eyes. She glanced up and watched a pelican dive for its breakfast, then come to rest on an old piling near the shore.

"It's not nearly as beautiful as you are, but it will do."

The sound of his voice startled her, and she turned her gaze to find him leaning against the boom, the breeze blowing through his thick hair, his naked torso gleaming beneath the sun. He'd been in the water, and his shorts clung to his skin, revealing narrow hips and muscled thighs. A shiver skittered down her spine, and she hugged herself.

"Where are we?"

He stretched his arms above his head and smiled. "It's called Bottle Key," he said, pushing his sunglasses up on his head. He met her gaze. "Are you feeling better?"

Carrie nodded, ignoring the current of attraction that sparked to life at the sight of him, the sound of his voice. "Thank you for the…the gifts," she said, shading her eyes as she stared at him. "It was very thoughtful of you."

She expected Dev to come nearer, but he maintained his spot on top of the forward cabin, his bare feet braced against the gentle rocking of the boat. Carrie swallowed hard, her mind searching for an appropriate topic of conversation. Finally, she conceded defeat. She couldn't think of a single thing that Dev Riley might find interesting. "It's a beautiful day." The weather was always a good topic. "Very…sunny."

"Did you sleep well?"

Carrie nodded. "Oh, very well. Like a rock. Out like a light. How about you?"

"I didn't think I would, but I did."

"Good," she said. "I—I'm glad I didn't keep you up."

"I'm not," he teased.

A long silence grew between them, and she shifted nervously, glancing back at Captain Fergus. What did Dev mean by that? Had he wanted to do more than just turn off the light and fall asleep? And if he had, then why *hadn't* he?

"I'm glad you're up," Dev finally said. "I wanted to talk to you." He held out his hand and helped her out of the cockpit onto the forward deck. She followed him to the bow of the boat, her mind focused on the feel of their fingers laced together, the warm strength of his hands. How would it feel to have those hands on her body, his palms covering her—

She cleared her throat and banished such crazy thoughts from her mind. They'd spent the night in the same bed, and he hadn't made a single move in that direction. "If it's about the bed, I—"

He turned and pressed his finger to her lips, then drew his hand away, leaving a warm brand on her mouth. For a fleeting instant, she wished he would kiss her and put an end to their stilted conversation. A kiss she could handle much more easily than words.

He sat down on the deck and leaned back, bracing himself on his elbows and turning his face up to the sun. She took the opportunity to study his face, to memorize his features at close range and imprint them on her brain. When he glanced up at her, she quickly sat down beside him and fiddled with the wide brim of her straw hat.

"Do you think a man and woman can be friends?" he asked. "I mean, without sexual attraction getting in the way?"

Carrie shrugged, confused by a question that seemed to come out of the blue. "I guess so. Why not?"

"Have you ever had any male friends? Guys that you never wanted to go to bed with?"

"Sure," Carrie lied. The truth was, there had been so few men in her life she hadn't had the luxury of developing friendships with them. And she hadn't really enjoyed going to bed with any of the men she'd been with, either. It had all been so nerve-racking and clumsy and...disappointing.

"I've never had a woman friend," he continued. "Never even tried. I'm not sure it's possible."

"I'm your friend," Carrie said with a crooked smile. "Sort of. And if you haven't noticed, I am a woman."

He turned, his gaze fixing on her mouth. "I've noticed. Believe me, I have."

Carrie turned to look out at the horizon, secretly satisfied with his offhand compliment and his fascination with her lips.

"If we're going to spend the rest of our vacation together," he said, "it's good that we're friends, don't you think?"

"But we're not going to spend our vacation together," Carrie murmured. "I'm going into town this afternoon to see if I can find a way back to Miami. There's supposed to be a bus that—"

"But I want you to stay."

Carrie's heart stopped, and for a moment she forgot to breathe. Could he really mean what he said? She wanted to trust his words, but her instincts told her to maintain her distance. Reality rarely measured up to fantasy. Dev Riley had already proved as much.

"It'll be good for me. To be around a woman and not think about—you know." He paused. "Besides, you paid for this vacation. It's not your fault someone screwed up. You have as much right to enjoy yourself as I do. So I want you to stay. I'd enjoy the company. And you can have the bed. I'll find another place to sleep."

Carrie felt her temper slowly rise. It was so nice to know that he could just put aside any attraction he might have for her! So reassuring to learn that she was so...forgettable. But then, next to the women Dev dated, she probably didn't stand a chance. That was the reality of Dev Riley. A reality she'd have to accept at face value.

"But you have a girlfriend," Carrie reminded him. "How would she feel about...this?"

A long silence grew between them. "Why would you think I have a girlfriend?" he asked.

Carrie cleared her throat nervously. She knew because Susie had told her. "I just assumed that..." She took a deep breath. "You booked a trip for two. You said so. And that first night, in bed. You thought I was someone else, didn't you? Someone more than a stranger. You thought I was her."

"Jillian," he replied, his voice suddenly cold.

"And why isn't she here? Shouldn't she be sharing your vacation with you? Instead of me?"

She sensed him tensing beside her and she cursed her curiosity. Didn't she have a right to know what had happened to Jillian? After all, she and Dev had shared a bed two nights in a row. And he'd asked her to spend the rest of the week with him. If he was still seriously involved, she needed to know.

"She's not here because she valued her career more than she did our relationship. It's all over between us." His reply sounded so matter-of-fact, shocking her with its suppressed anger and bitterness.

Carrie pulled her knees up under her chin and tipped her face up into the breeze. Her heart skipped at this revelation, but she chose to ignore it. The news should make no difference at all. But it did cause her spirits to brighten a bit. "I'm sorry," she lied.

"I'm not. It's for the best. I don't need a woman in my life right now. Believe me, I'll be better off without her."

As quickly as her spirits had soared, they came crashing back to earth. He didn't need a woman in his life, yet he'd just asked her to spend his vacation with him. What did he think she was? Some sexless mutant alien? She was a woman with hormones, with normal needs, with passions and desires that could become inflamed by such close proximity to a handsome man!

"It's more ego than regret," he continued. "She wasn't ready to commit, and neither was I. I'm just angry that she realized it before I did."

Carrie glanced over at him. Had she been as sophisticated and worldly as Jillian, she might possess the techniques to make him see her as an object of desire rather than a—a traveling companion. But she wasn't Jillian, that much remained patently obvious.

"So will you stay?" he asked.

Carrie nodded and pushed to her feet. "Sure. No problem." She smoothed her dress and forced a smile. "Fergus and Moira offered to take me over to the village after lunch. Would you like to come?"

He shook his head. "Naw. I think I'll stay on board. Maybe take a swim, do some reading. Go ahead. Enjoy yourself." He leaned back and closed his eyes again. She waited for a few minutes, then silently moved along the rail to the cabin hatchway. When she regained the safety of her cabin, she sat down on the edge of the bed and tried to put some order to her confusion. After such a baffling conversation, she only knew one thing for sure.

It was much easier to hate Dev Riley when he acted like a cad.

CARRIE SAT IN THE BOW of the dinghy and stared at *Serendipity* as it rocked against its anchor in the secluded cove. When she'd emerged from her cabin before lunch, Dev had been gone. Captain Fergus had told her that he had ferried him over to town in the dinghy. Dev had promised to meet Fergus at the dock later that afternoon for a ride back.

Carrie spent the rest of the morning reading and waiting for him to return, but when it looked as if she'd be eating lunch alone, she decided to accompany Moira and Fergus into the small town of Tavernier on Key Largo. It was silly to waste time thinking about Dev, when she could be prowling the tiny shops that lined the harbor. To her surprise, she enjoyed her solitary explorations and reveled in her newfound confidence. Traveling alone wasn't nearly as awful as she'd thought it would be.

Tavernier was a bustling little village with a pretty harbor. When they arrived, Moira and Fergus set off to find a new halyard for the jib at a marina on the other side of the key. Carrie arranged to meet them at the dinghy in two hours, then set off on the narrow street that rose up from the waterfront.

The street was warm from the sun, and the soft ocean breeze fluttered the awnings over the shop windows. A scruffy little dog fell into step beside her, waiting patiently for her while she shopped. At Mississippi Mac's, an open-air tavern right on the waterfront, she found a table and ordered some deep-fried shrimp. She fed the little dog tidbits as she sipped a cool rum punch and watched the passersby—

A shrill whistle split the air, and Carrie turned to look out from beneath the awning.

"Aggie! You little tramp, where are you?"

She turned back to her dinner, uninterested in a stranger's domestic problems. But a few moments later, a shadow darkened her table. Carrie looked up from her food. Against the glare of the sun, she could see the silhouette of a man, broadshouldered and shirtless, his long hair whipping in the wind. She shaded her eyes with her hand. For a moment, she thought it was Dev, until he spoke.

"Aggie, you know you're not supposed to beg." His Australian accent gave his words an odd cadence, and at first she didn't understand what he'd said.

"I'm afraid you've mistaken me for someone else," Carrie murmured nervously. "I'm not Aggie."

The man pulled out the chair next to her, flipped it around and straddled it. Her breath caught in her throat, and she swallowed hard as her gaze came to rest on the bronzed Adonis who sat next to her. His skin was golden brown, his hair streaked blond by the sun. His profile was startling in its perfection: a straight nose, high cheekbones and a strong jaw. Though he wasn't nearly as handsome as Dev, she had to admit that he wasn't hard to look at. He smiled and tipped his head toward the little dog. "Of course you aren't Aggie. But he is."

Carrie frowned.

"My dog," he explained. "His name is Aggie. And you must be Fergus and Moira's passenger." He reached over the table. "Name's Jace Stevens. Sydney, Australia."

Carrie hesitantly reached out and took his hand. "Carrie. Carrie Reynolds. Lake Grove, Ill—I mean, Montana. So, you know Captain Fergus and Moira?"

The man nodded. "We run into each other all the time in different ports around the Caribbean. I've know them for years. I saw them over at the marina, and Moira told me they had a charter. A pretty young lady, she said. And when I saw you, I knew that lady had to be you."

Carrie felt the heat rise in her cheeks and she

dropped her gaze to her food. *A pretty young lady?* That was the second time in a day that a man had commented on her beauty. First Dev, and now this stranger. Did the spots on her face somehow make her irresistible to the opposite sex? Or were men in the Florida Keys particularly desperate?

"Thank you," she murmured, uneasy with compliments. Carrie swallowed hard and tried to think of something to say. After all, this is what she'd come on vacation for—social interaction with the opposite sex. Now was the time to practice! "Then you're a charter captain, too, Mr. Stevens?" she ventured.

Good question, Carrie thought, her mind racing to anticipate the next subject and her response. She'd just ask him to talk about himself. She'd read somewhere that men liked that. Carrie groaned inwardly. Why couldn't conversation come more naturally to her? She felt as breathless as if she were in the midst of a marathon.

He cupped his chin in his hand and shook his head. "No, just a boat rat. I spend winters down here, and summers on the racing circuit up north. What do you do in Lake Grove, Montana?"

"You race cars?" she asked, steering the conversation back to him, and rather proud of her effort.

He chuckled, his white teeth gleaming in the sun. "No, sailboats. Big sailboats. Twelve-meter yachts. Like the kind they sail in the America's Cup."

Carrie groaned inwardly. Twelve-meter yachts. Now there's a subject she knew absolutely nothing about. "It's hard for me to imagine racing a sailboat. Like racing turtles, isn't it? They don't go very fast."

He leaned over and grinned. "You ought to try it sometime. There's nothing like it. The wind in your hair, the sails snapping overhead. It's better than sex."

Carrie clasped her hands in front of her. If she didn't know better, she'd swear the man was intent on charming her! A perfect stranger comes up to her at a sidewalk café and starts a conversation—using his cute little dog to run interference! He was shameless—and sexy. And obviously interested. But why?

He didn't look that desperate. She studied him covertly as she took another sip of her drink. Maybe it was the new hair color or the sundress that revealed just enough cleavage to be enticing. Or did she somehow exude a newfound confidence with the opposite sex? Whatever it was, Carrie was enjoying the attention. And what harm could come of it? She was on vacation. And the man was a friend of Fergus and Moira, a couple she trusted.

"I'd probably throw up," Carrie admitted. "Fergus and Moira probably told you that I'm not much of a sailor."

"That can't be true," he teased, reaching down to pat his dog on the head. "Aggie knows a good sailor when he sees one. Would you like to see my boat? I'm anchored in the harbor."

Carrie shook her head, then glanced at her watch. "I can't. I have to meet Moira and Fergus."

"Why don't you stay and have another drink with me? I'll sail you back to *Serendipity* later."

The brief flirtation had gone well, but Carrie wasn't sure that she was ready to move on to drinks and more intimate conversation, especially with a man she really didn't know. She placed her napkin on the table and slid back in her chair. "They're expecting me."

He stood and held out his hand. "Then Aggie and I will walk you back down to the harbor."

A familiar male voice joined the conversation. "I'll walk her back."

Carrie glanced over her shoulder to see Dev standing behind her. He wore a pair of baggy shorts and a pale blue T-shirt, the color of the sea. His hair was windblown, yet still damp at his nape, and his eyes were fixed on Jace Stevens and narrowed with suspicion.

Carrie cleared her throat, then quickly stood, uneasy with Dev's edgy mood. "Dev Riley, I'd like to introduce a friend of the O'Malleys. This is—"

"We have to go," Dev interrupted. He reached down and took her hand, then tossed a few bills on the table. He gave Jace a curt nod before he led Carrie toward the street.

"I was just going to introduce you to—"

"We have to go!" he repeated, more insistently. "Moira and Fergus are waiting."

Carrie turned back and gave Jace Stevens a little wave. "It was nice meeting you," she called. "Bye, Aggie!"

"Don't talk to him," Dev muttered, tugging at her arm. "You'll only encourage him. Guys like that don't know when to quit."

"He's a nice man," Carrie countered.

"He's a stranger, and you don't talk to strangers."

"He's not a stranger. He knows Fergus and Moira."

"Maybe you talk to strangers in Helena, but not here. He could be a...a drug runner. Or a criminal on the lam. Or—or a pirate."

Carrie laughed, yanking her arm from his hand. "A pirate? Are you crazy? He races sailboats."

He gave her a sideways glance, his jaw tight. "Dammit, you know what I'm saying, Carrie."

She hurried to catch up with his long stride. "I know what you're saying, but I'm not sure why you're saying it. Who are you to tell me who I can and cannot talk to? Just because you're my friend, doesn't mean you can boss me around."

"I'm simply concerned for your safety," he said, his gaze fixed straight ahead.

"Maybe you're just jealous," she muttered.

He stopped in the middle of the street, grabbed her hand, and faced her. "What? What did you say?"

Carrie's gaze dropped to her toes and she kicked at a pebble. "Nothing."

"No, you said something. What was it?"

Planting her fists on her hips, Carrie tipped her chin up and met his angry gaze. "I said, maybe you're jealous."

"Of that bum? Ha! You're dreaming. I could buy and sell that guy a million times over."

Her eyebrow arched and she sent him her most disdainful look. "How nice to know that." She set back off toward the waterfront. "All I was doing was talking. He was quite charming. It was an enlightening experience."

"Is that what you call it? He was trying to pick you up."

"Listen, you may be blessed with an abundance of charm, but I haven't had much experience at this. That's why I came on vacation. To practice." As soon as the words were out of her mouth, she regretted saying them.

"To practice seducing strangers at a bar?"

"He wasn't a stranger, and I was sitting at a restaurant, not a bar. There was no seduction involved."

"Then what were you practicing for?"

Carrie drew a deep breath and tried to calm her temper. "It's none of your business what I'm practicing for."

"It's my business when you put yourself in danger," he insisted.

"That man was a friend of Fergus and Moira. I wasn't in any danger! Now can we stop talking about this?"

"You are too naive for your own good, Carrie," he muttered, starting toward the boat again. "You're not in Helena anymore. And it's plain to see that you don't have much experience with men."

Carrie gasped. "Well, maybe I don't. But I'm not going to get any experience if I don't practice!"

"Who are you practicing for?"

"I can't tell you," Carrie said, pulling away from him and quickening her pace.

He caught up to her in three short steps, blocking her way with his body. "Tell me," he demanded. "We're supposed to be friends, aren't we? You can trust me."

Carrie nearly laughed at the absurdity of it all. What did he want to hear? That she'd come on this vacation to become the kind of woman *he* could fall for? That she'd been set on having a torrid tropical fling before heading home? "All right! There is this man," she finally said. "He doesn't even know I exist."

After a long silence, he tipped her chin up and looked into her eyes. "How could anyone not know you exist?" he asked, his voice soft.

Carrie shot him a sardonic smile, ignoring the tiny thrill that raced through her. "Hard to believe," she said. "But true."

"Do you love him?"

The question took her by surprise. Four days ago, Dev Riley had been nothing more than a fantasy. It had been so much easier to discount her feelings for him then. But now that she knew him, the feelings were so much more real. Whether it was love or not, she wasn't sure. But she was beginning to feel something, deep in her heart, something that stirred her soul and drew them closer.

Carrie took a shaky breath. "No," she said, her voice wavering. "I don't love him." She glanced up and met his gaze, his green eyes filled with concern. "All right. Maybe. A little."

"Then let *me* help you," he said. "Not some stranger you find in a bar."

"How can you help?"

"If you want to practice on someone, practice on me. And then I'll know you're safe."

Carrie shook her head. Safe? Practicing her seduction techniques with Dev Riley? "Thanks for the offer," she said. "But I don't think that would be such a good idea. Besides, why are you worried about my safety?"

"Because we're friends. And that's what friends do. They watch out for each other."

Carrie stared at him for a long moment, her eyes taking in the firm set of his mouth, his unyielding expression. This was all she needed: an open invitation to lust after her ultimate fantasy man. It was bad enough that they'd agreed to spend the week together, but now he was offering her the opportunity to hone her social skills on the very person she was practicing for!

This was not going to work, Carrie mused. It could only lead to disaster. But then, this whole trip had been a disaster, hadn't it? At least this particular catastrophe would be worth remembering once she got back home.

SERENDIPITY CUT SMOOTHLY through calm seas, her bow creating a white wake in the dark water. Dev braced his shoulder on the mast and looked up at the night sky, glittering with stars that he'd never seen before and a moon so bright that it lit the sails above his head. In the distance he could see lights from a village on the main highway; the inhabitants were obviously sound asleep, unaware of their silent passing.

He could almost imagine how these waters had been a few hundred years ago. Over dinner that night, Captain Fergus had regaled them with tales of pirates and wreckers, adventurers and settlers. He'd even told them a ghost story about a group of railroad workers who had been swept away during a hurricane, and now haunted the waters with their cries for help.

Carrie had listened raptly to all the stories, but had said little to Dev. She picked at her dinner of grilled snapper and made polite conversation, but Dev could tell that she'd been uneasy over her earlier revelations. His thoughts returned to their conversation on the street above the harbor. He hadn't meant to get angry with Carrie, but seeing her with another guy had just set him off. In any other man, it might have seemed like jealousy, but Dev knew he didn't have a jealous bone in his body. Instead, he brushed off his feelings as a simple need to protect a friend...a *good* friend...a friend he'd grown quite fond of over the past few days.

He'd tried to sleep in the small cabin, but after only a few minutes, he found himself on deck. Dev drew a deep breath of the cool night air and closed his eyes, pushing thoughts of Carrie—and the man she loved—out of his mind. But it was no use. An image of the guy flashed before his eyes, and it was an image that he found downright annoying. His imagination probably had nothing to do with reality, but he pictured the rugged cowboy type, the kind that populated a place like Helena, the type of man that all women found attractive—especially an innocent like Carrie.

He cursed silently. He couldn't begin to understand the attraction. What did some cowboy from Montana have that Dev didn't—besides a horse and a pair of well-worn cowboy boots? Did he have an MBA from Northwestern? Could he run a multinational corporation? Did he even know what a leveraged buyout was?

Dev's jaw grew tight. Obviously, Carrie had settled for the first man she'd been attracted to. She was too besotted to see the problems inherent in such an ill-advised liaison. After all, there were the long cattle drives and the rowdy evenings spent at the local saloon, not to mention the overpowering smell of sweaty horses and cow manure. A relationship like that was doomed from the start. And as her friend and confidant, it was his responsibility to convince her of this fact.

Dev cursed silently. Was he really concerned about her welfare? Or was he just using that as an excuse to ignore feelings that came perilously close to jealousy? He'd already resolved to keep his relationship with Carrie strictly platonic. But then, that was easier to accomplish in theory than it was in practice. In fact, everything became so much more confusing when he stared into her pretty blue eyes.

She had asked for his help, and as a proper friend, he was obliged to give it. Dev raked his hands through his damp hair. But was he really a proper friend? A friend shouldn't fantasize about kissing her. But he did. He shouldn't feel such an overpowering need to touch her. Yet he did. And more and more lately, his thoughts had turned to things much more intimate, much more passionate than just a simple kiss or a brief caress.

So why had he offered to help her "practice"? At every turn, his resolve would be tested. A smile curled his lips. He had to appreciate her naiveté. Carrie had no understanding of her own beauty.

Her motives, unlike his, were entirely pure. Though he'd only known her a few days, he could be certain that she'd never resort to the typical feminine tricks, the manipulation and the flattery that worked on so many men.

No, once she set her mind to snaring her cowboy, it would take little more than a coy smile and a few soft words. After all, that's all she'd had to do to capture his heart. And Dev's heart had been well hardened by Jillian and her lot.

A movement caught his eye, and he turned to see Carrie walking along the rail to the bow of the boat. She wore the white nightgown he'd purchased for her. The breeze set it billowing around her legs, and for an instant, she looked like an angel floating to earth in the moonlight. At first, he thought she'd seen him. But when she passed without glancing his way, he realized she was oblivious to his presence.

He held his breath and watched as she looked out to sea, her face turned up to the soft spray that kicked up over the bow. She reached up and ran her fingers through her hair, then stretched her arms over her head. The bow light created a soft halo around her body, and he could see the outline of her form beneath the translucent fabric: her ripe breasts, her lush hips, the perfect curve of her backside.

His fingers clenched, and he felt himself grow hard with desire. He could imagine brushing the nightgown off her shoulders and letting it flutter down around her feet. Her skin would be warm and smooth, and his palms would explore every sweet inch of her flesh. She'd respond to his touch, and they'd lie down on the smooth deck, beneath the stars and the moon. They'd make love, the sea rushing past them, the warm salt air cooling their naked bodies.

He closed his eyes and drew a deep breath. What was it that drew him to her? What was this irresistible, yet unseen force that pulled him toward such a tantalizing prize? And why Carrie? Why now? The last thing he wanted in his life was another woman, another chance at confusion and frustration. He wanted things to be simple again.

But wanting Carrie *was* simple! She was sweet and pure and honest. Even though he'd known her only a few short days, he could trust her. Though she might attempt to hide her emotions, she was perfectly transparent, her every feeling and fear reflected in her pretty eyes.

He'd seen desire there, too, when he'd kissed her. He'd also detected confusion and regret. He wanted her in a way that he'd never wanted a woman before—total possession, complete surrender. But she loved another man. Was he willing to ignore that fact to satisfy his own baser needs?

Maybe the situation wasn't quite as clear as it seemed on the surface, he mused. She was in love, but the guy didn't know she existed. That meant there was no prior commitment. And Dev was free of any entanglements. They were both adults, both capable of making their own decisions. Why not let events lead where they might?

Lots of people had vacation love affairs, then went back home to their day-to-day existence without a second thought or a moment's regret. He'd go back to his work, and she'd go back to her cowboy—both of them content with the memories of their week together....

He frowned. Somehow, he sensed that forgetting Carrie would be far easier said than done.

He closed his eyes and leaned against the mast, letting the night wind buffet his body. Her image danced in his brain, teasing and taunting him, the nightgown slowly dissolving in his imagination until she stood naked before him, a sea siren drawing him into her domain.

When he looked over at the bow again, she was gone. Dev shook his head and rubbed his eyes. Had he only imagined her there? Had his addled brain manufactured her image to satisfy some unbidden desire? Or was he simply tired? With a silent oath, Dev made his way along the rail, then down into the main saloon. When he reached the door of his berth, he paused. The tiny cabin was close and airless, and he couldn't help but think about Carrie, lying in her big, comfortable bed, while just a thin bulkhead separated the two of them. Dev took a step toward the forward cabin, and then another.

He wanted to talk to her, needed to see her again before he slept. He listened at the door for a long moment, then pushed it open. The cabin was dark, and he could see her form on the bed, outlined by the moonlight that streamed through the portholes. Her soft breathing—slow and even—was the only sound that touched his ears. He fought the urge to walk over to the bed and crawl in beside her, to complete what he'd started that first night.

Would she respond to his touch? Or would she pull away? He wanted to make love to her, to possess her body and touch her soul. But he knew Carrie's heart was more fragile than most. She longed for true and everlasting romance with her cowboy, not a one-night stand with a virtual stranger.

She moaned softly and then mumbled in her sleep. Dev held his breath and listened, but soon she quieted. He crossed the cabin and stood beside the bed. Her curly hair fanned out across her pillow, and he reached down to take a strand between his fingers.

"Dev," she murmured. "Umm, Dev."

He snatched his hand away and pressed his palm against his chest. His heart thudded beneath his fingertips. Slowly, she opened her eyes. At first, he thought she was asleep, still caught in the dream she was having. But then, Carrie frowned and pushed up on her elbow, brushing her hair out of her eyes.

"Dev?"

"I—I didn't mean to wake you," he murmured, stepping back. "I was looking for—for my—for something I lost. My book."

"Is everything all right?"

"I couldn't sleep."

She sighed softly, then reached over and grabbed the covers, pulling them back in a silent invitation. "Get the cushions," she murmured. "You can sleep with me."

Every instinct told him to walk out of the cabin right then. There was no way he could spend another night in her bed without touching her, without curling up against her soft body and burying his face in her fragrant hair, without peeling the clothes from her body and—

"It's all right," she murmured. "I don't mind. I trust you."

He grabbed the cushions and tossed them down on the bed, then stretched out beside them. For a long time, the cabin was silent, and he waited for her to say something, to give him an opening, a sign that she might share in his desires. Finally, he rolled to his side, took her face between his hands and kissed her hard on the mouth.

"Good night, Carrie." With a long sigh, he laid back and smiled, folding his hands on his chest. Now *she'd* have something to keep her awake the rest of the night, and he'd be the one to get a good night's sleep. And in the morning, he'd try to figure out just what the hell he was going to do about Carrie Reynolds.

5

CARRIE REYNOLDS STARED into the mirror, carefully evaluating her case of sun poisoning. The spots were gone and her complexion had taken on a healthy glow. The only remnants of another night spent in bed with Dev Riley were the dark circles under her eyes and the tingle that touched her lips every time she thought about his kiss.

As kisses go, it wasn't very romantic. He had taken her by surprise, so much so that she'd barely had time to react, and no time to evaluate his intent. She must have done something to make him want to kiss her, but she couldn't recall what it was. She hadn't said anything, or acted as if she wanted to be kissed. Had she known what precipitated the whole thing, she might be able to repeat it, because she surely did want Dev Riley to kiss her again.

Carrie reached for her lipstick and pulled off the cap, then stopped. Dev had made his feelings perfectly clear yesterday. They were friends—traveling companions and nothing more. But friends kissed each other on the cheek, not on the mouth. And friends slept in separate beds. The bounds of their "friendship" seemed to change at his slightest whim.

She carefully applied the lipstick and tossed it

back in her bag, then ran her fingers through her tangled hair. If she'd had more experience with men, she might be able to read the signs a little better. "Whatever happens," she murmured, "will be good practice—for all those other men out there waiting for me." After all, that's why she'd come on this trip. To make herself more interesting. And what better way to do that than to experience all the delights the Florida Keys had to offer—including an occasional kiss from Dev Riley?

She rubbed her tired eyes. "I need some coffee," she said.

Carrie grabbed the blanket and wrapped it around her shoulders. She'd have her coffee in her cabin, as she dressed. But when she crawled out on deck, Moira and Captain Fergus were nowhere to be found. Nor was Dev. She glanced around the boat, then realized that they were no longer underway. The horizon wasn't moving, and the boat wasn't rocking.

Serendipity gently drifted with the wind, pulling against its anchor line. Over the bow, she could see the shoreline, with its narrow sand beach and thick mangrove forest beyond. Carrie called out, but no one answered. She made her way back to the rear deck where they usually enjoyed their meals, and found a carafe of coffee and a selection of pastries and fresh fruit.

As she munched on a croissant, she stared out across the azure water. It was a perfect day, the sky as blue as—

Her gaze landed on something in the water off starboard. A body! Floating face down in the water.

"Hey!" Carrie glanced around, then leaned over the rail. She recognized the blue shorts and the dark hair. It wasn't just *any* body in the water. "Dev!" He didn't move; his legs hung beneath the surface, his arms outspread. Her mind screamed with the possibilities. He'd drowned while she'd been sleeping the morning away. Or maybe he had been attacked by a shark, while she'd perfected the application of her lipstick. Or it could have been one of those poisonous fishes. Or he could have hit his head on a rock, or jumped in the water too soon after eating breakfast.

Carrie scurried around the deck, looking for something to toss into the water. She heaved a seat cushion over the rail, then another, then tossed out two of the rubber bumpers that protected the boat's hull from the edge of the dock. But her aim was off, and the body remained immobile, now floating away from her. By the time she grabbed the life ring from the stern of the boat, Carrie knew she'd have to jump in and swim out to him.

"If you don't want to drown, don't go near the water," she muttered, her voice trembling. She'd never been a strong swimmer, and the shore seemed so far off. But the water wasn't that deep, and if she held on to the life ring, maybe she'd be able to get to Dev in time. She dropped the blanket and slipped the ring around her waist. Drawing a long breath, she perched on the stern and gathered her courage, then began to crawl down the ladder.

Her nightgown billowed out around her, floating on the surface. The shock of the cool water creeping up her bare skin frightened her at first, but once she was certain she'd float, Carrie let go of the ladder and began to kick toward Dev. "You can do this," she murmured, her heart racing and her breath coming in soft gasps. But what would she do when she got to him? Would she have the strength to haul him back to the boat and drag him on board? Could she remember how to do mouth-to-mouth resuscitation? And what if he was dead? Oh, where were Fergus and Moira?

Carrie groaned and paddled faster. She was nearly there, her fingertips just inches from his head. Suddenly, he popped up out of the water so fast that she screamed. A scuba mask covered his eyes, and for the first time, she noticed the breathing tube tucked over his ear. Dev pushed the mask on top of his head and grinned. "Morning."

A vivid oath sprung from her lips, and she slapped her hand on the water, showering him with droplets. "I thought you were dead!"

He slicked his hair back and blinked in confusion. "What?"

Carrie couldn't control her temper. "How could you be so irresponsible? Swimming alone is dangerous. Where is Captain Fergus? And Moira?"

Dev wiped the water from his eyes, at first surprised, then amused by her futile flailing. He grabbed her around the waist and pulled her against him. "They took the dinghy and went across the channel to Little Torch Key. What are you so angry about?"

"I saw you from the boat and I thought you'd drowned. You were so still."

"You were trying to save me?" He glanced over her shoulder. "Is that why half the cushions are floating around the boat?"

Carrie pressed her hands against his bare chest, feeling the play of muscle beneath the smooth, sunburnished skin. She left them there just a few seconds longer than she should have before pushing him away. "You weren't moving. I didn't know what to do. I—I panicked."

"I was just snorkeling. There's a nice reef out here. I was watching a manta ray and didn't want to scare him off."

Carrie snaked her arms around his neck and wrapped her legs around his waist. "A manta ray? That's not poisonous, is it?"

He slid his hands along the outside of her thighs. "No. And it's long gone. You scared him off with all your flailing."

Untangling her legs from around him, she pushed away again. "You saw me swimming toward you, and you didn't come up?"

Dev chuckled. "I was enjoying the view beneath the surface. You have beautiful legs, Carrie Reynolds." He looked down through the crystal clear water and shook his head in mock amazement. "Incredible legs. And I like the lacy underwear, too."

Carrie reached down and pushed at the hem of her nightgown, but it kept floating up around her, exposing her legs and panties. "I could have drowned. I'm not a strong swimmer, you know."

"Are you saying you risked your life for me? A mere acquaintance? The guy who'd steal your bed the moment you let your guard down?"

She narrowed her eyes. "Next time I won't be so quick to jump in the water. I'll leave you to the sharks." He smiled at that, and Carrie realized that this had been that witty banter that she'd so admired in other women—a flirtatious little technique that she'd never been able to master. But suddenly, she was able to match him, word for word. And they were both enjoying themselves.

He reached out and brushed a strand of hair from her cheek. "You look pretty when you're all wet," he murmured. His hands moved over her body, around her waist, skimming her hips. Carrie trembled in anticipation. How could he touch her like this and not feel just a tiny flash of desire? She risked a glance up, and what she saw caused her pulse to jump.

He stared down at her, his green eyes dark with intent, his gaze fixed on her mouth. She willed him to kiss her the same way he had last night, only longer and deeper. A lazy kiss that would make her mind go numb and her fingers tingle.

Dev bent nearer, and she held her breath. Now she felt as if *she* were drowning, desire welling up around her until an uneasy panic set in. Carrie wasn't sure what to say, how to act. But once again, she'd sent him some silent signal, for a soft moan sprang from his throat and he pulled her into his arms.

They floated in the water; his mouth was warm on her wet skin. His lips traced a path along her jaw, down her neck to the angle of her collarbone, to the spot where her pulse fluttered. Heat seeped through her limbs, and she felt weightless, as the gentle waves pushed her against his lean, muscular body, then pulled her away.

Their hips met, then parted, then met again, hinting at what they might share if their passion overcame them both. The hard ridge of his desire branded her flesh through the fabric of her nightgown, and she wanted to touch him there, to wrap her fingers around his need.

His hands slid down along her hips, and he cupped her backside in his palms and drew her thighs up around his waist. Carrie had never felt so alive, yet so completely lost. Every sensation was new and impossibly arousing. His lips returned to hers and he explored her mouth with his tongue, gently at first and then with an intensity that threatened to render her unconscious. She groaned softly, and he drew away. "I could teach you," he murmured, tracing her lower lip with his thumb. "It's not difficult."

Carrie blinked. "W-was I that bad?"

"It's easier if you don't work so hard. Just relax."

"I am relaxed. Very...relaxed."

"I'm a certified instructor. I have been since high school. I've taught a lot of people."

She frowned. "To kiss?"

Dev laughed. He let go of her and began to stroke a lazy circle around her, splashing water at her playfully. "No, silly girl! To swim. I could teach you to swim. You already know how to kiss."

But she didn't want to practice swimming; she wanted to continue kissing Dev! How could he just switch gears so quickly, from swimming to kissing to swimming again? "I don't think so," Carrie replied. "I'm not very athletic. Every time I try, I sink like a stone."

He spread his hands around her waist. "Take off

the life preserver. We'll have our first lesson right now. Payback for saving my life."

"I really can't." She paused. "I didn't bring along a swimsuit."

"You come to the Caribbean and you forget your swimsuit and your sunscreen." He sent her a devastating grin. "You don't have a clue how to travel, do you? What am I going to do with you, Carrie Reynolds?"

You could kiss me again, Carrie wanted to say. *You could touch me and make me feel like my skin is on fire. You could drag me out of the water and make love to me on the beach the way Burt Lancaster did with Deborah Kerr.*

"The truth is, I haven't traveled much," she finally said. "My mom died when I was young, and I took care of my dad all during high school and college. Then after I graduated, I worked at building my business."

"In Helena," he added.

"Helena?"

"Yeah. Montana. You told me the first night. Remember?"

Carrie forced a smile. "Oh, yes. Helena."

"The capital of Montana. The Treasure State." He winked. "See, if you can teach me the state capitals, I can teach you how to swim."

"I guess you could," she murmured.

"Trust me." With that, he carefully slipped the life ring over her head. As soon as it was gone, she felt herself sinking. Carrie slipped her arms around his shoulders and hung on. Her breasts pressed against his chest, the thin fabric of her gown now an unwanted barrier. She longed to feel nothing between them but the warm water, to put her lips on his chest and taste the salt on his skin. Had she been braver, she might have pulled the hem of her gown up and over her head, but the thought of such a bold move made her head spin and her confidence flag. She held her breath and tried to calm her racing heart.

"We'll start with floating," he murmured. "Tip your head back. Arch your neck." He held his hands in the small of her back, and she felt her body bob to the surface. "Point your toes. Now, take a deep breath and stick your chest out."

Carrie kicked her feet and sank back down into the water, grabbing hold of his neck again. "What is this? You're not teaching me how to float! You are such a fiend."

He blinked in surprise. "I swear, that's what you have to do."

She glared at him suspiciously. "Are you sure?"

Dev nodded and pushed her away, slowly helping her back to where she'd stopped. "Put your arms out," he said.

His quiet and patient instructions lulled her into a relaxing sense of security. She stared up at the sky and listened to his soothing voice. His hands gradually drew away, and a tiny smile curled her lips as she floated on the surface of the water. She wasn't afraid, even though the water was over her head and the shore was a long swim away. Dev would save her if she started to drown.

As she relaxed, her mind drifted back to the feel of his hands on her body...so firm and sure. What would it be like to have him touch her with unbridled intent? He always stopped just as her own desire peaked; he was always in control. How would it be if just once he didn't stop? A delicious warmth worked its way through her limbs.

Just a few days ago, Dev Riley seemed so far out of reach—a fantasy man she could never hope to have. And now, here she was, so far from her day-to-day existence, talking to him, touching him, trusting him. What had happened to her? Had she become a different person the minute she stepped on board *Serendipity?* Or had she simply blossomed beneath the warm sun? She could talk to him the way she'd never been able to talk to a man before. And she felt a need stronger than she ever could have imagined.

Carrie closed her eyes and listened to the quiet, even sound of her breathing. Weightless, suspended in the warm water, all her doubts and fears seemed to float away. She sighed softly. It would be so easy to tempt him, to test his resolve. And what did she have to lose? Once she went home, she'd never have to talk to him again. If she made a fool of herself in the attempt, she could put it all behind her and go back to being the Carrie Reynolds she'd always been—mousy hair, bland wardrobe, boring life.

There was no risk, no downside...except that she'd probably destroy their newfound friendship. But was it friendship she really wanted to take away from this vacation? Or was it memories of a single passionate night with Dev Riley?

DEV SAT ON THE DECK of the boat, his legs hanging over the side. He took a slow sip of his beer and looked over at Carrie. She lay on the foredeck, protected from the sun by the canopy he'd draped from the mast to the bow rail. Her eyes were closed, and he suspected she was asleep.

She'd swum for nearly an hour, and by the time they had finished he'd turned her into a passable swimmer. It was nice to have something to offer a woman. Jillian had been so independent. She made her own money, her own decisions. Even when he had offered advice or an opinion, he got the distinct impression that Jillian wasn't really listening.

But the simple act of teaching Carrie to swim had brought him undeniable pleasure. She enjoyed little things—a shell he retrieved from the beach that she still held clutched in her hand, a drink he'd brought her when they came back on board, the canopy he'd put up to protect her delicate skin from the tropical sun. Any act of kindness was met with a sweet smile.

Dev's gaze drifted down from her mouth along the length of her body. She hadn't bothered to change out of her nightgown. Perhaps she might have, had she realized that it became nearly transparent when wet. The damp fabric still clung to her skin, outlining the perfect curves of her breasts, revealing the dusty-rose color of her nipples and the shadow of the panties she wore.

He drew a deep breath, then let it out slowly. A friendship with Carrie Reynolds had seemed like a practical goal for his vacation. But from the moment he'd made the suggestion, Dev had found good cause to question his sanity. How the hell was he supposed to keep her at arm's length when she kept falling into his arms at the slightest cause?

How odd that he found her so captivating. Had

anyone told him he'd find himself attracted to such a simple and guileless woman, he might have brushed off the suggestion as absurd. But every time he turned around, she was there, unwittingly testing his resolve, tempting him with her sweet mouth and her lush body.

"Ahoy, there!"

Dev drew his eyes away from Carrie, and turned to see Fergus and Moira approaching the boat in the dinghy. He pressed his index finger to his lips and pointed to Carrie.

Fergus gave him a nod and Moira smiled as they quietly maneuvered the dinghy around to the stern. Fergus killed the outboard, tied up, then hefted a few bags of groceries up to Dev. He helped his wife back on board before nimbly jumping on behind her. "You've had a nice mornin' then?" he asked.

Dev nodded. "Very nice. I did some snorkeling, and Carrie learned to swim."

A knowing smile curled Moira's lips. "She did? And would you be her teacher then?"

"Moira McGuire O'Malley!" Fergus cried. "You stop that right now." He turned to Dev. "My wife fancies herself a bit of a matchmaker. You'll have to forgive her. I told her there was nothin' between the two of you, but she has other ideas."

Moira frowned at her husband, then grabbed the bag of groceries from his arms. "Had I waited for you to come callin', Fergus O'Malley, I'd be an old maid. I know a good match when I see one." With that, she sniffed disdainfully, then disappeared into the rear cabin. A few moments later, the sound of pots slamming against pans drifted up from the galley.

"She has it in her mind that there's something goin' on between you two," Captain Fergus explained. "I don't know where that woman gets her ideas, but I explained that you and Ms. Reynolds share no fond feelings for each other."

"No," Dev said distractedly. "We're just... friends."

"And I know Ms. Reynolds wants to get off the boat as soon as she can, so she can get on with that vacation she was promised."

Dev hesitated. He didn't like the direction this conversation was taking. "Maybe she does. I don't know. She hasn't said."

"I spoke with friends over on Little Torch Key. They're driving back into Miami this afternoon. I asked if they'd take Ms. Reynolds in to the airport, and they said they would." He glanced in her direction. "Or she can wait until tomorrow. We'll be in Key West, and there's an airport there. If she doesn't want to fly in a small plane, there's also an airport shuttle she can take back to Miami."

Dev shook his head. "Actually, I think she's decided to stay."

Fergus's eyebrow arched. "She has? But I thought she was—"

"No," Dev interrupted. "We've called a truce. There's no reason two adults can't spend a pleasant vacation together without it turning romantic. Right?"

Fergus's other eyebrow shot up, turning his expression to one of disbelief. He chuckled. "Have you ever been on vacation before, young man?"

"Yes. No," he amended, "not exactly. I've traveled, if that's what you're asking. But I've never really taken a vacation."

"I've been sailing folks around these islands for more years than I care to count," Fergus said. "And if I only know one thing, I know that these waters, these Florida Keys, have a way of changin' people. When a person forgets their troubles for a week or two, they leave room for more intriguing possibilities. Love, for one."

"We're not going to fall in love," Dev said, forcing a smile. "We barely know each other."

"I knew Moira was the gal for me the minute I first saw her. Love at first sight."

Dev considered his words for a long moment. Maybe if he were a sentimental fool, he might believe Captain Fergus. But he knew that love wasn't something that came quickly or easily. He and Jillian had known each other for two years before they'd even broached the subject. And then, their feelings for each other hadn't withstood the very first test.

"I'm not planning on falling in love with Carrie Reynolds," he insisted.

"Plans have nothin' to do with it," Fergus said, clapping him on the shoulder. "By the way, if you're so set on not fallin' in love, maybe you shouldn't spend a couple days on a romantic island with a pretty girl. Maybe you should be the one takin' that ride back to Miami before we get to Cristabel Key."

Dev watched the captain make his way through the hatch to his cabin, before turning back to Carrie. Maybe he should tell her about the ride back to

Miami. Given the choice, she might want to leave. She'd tried once before. What made him think that she'd changed her mind?

He tipped his head back and sighed. He hadn't misread the desire he'd seen in her blue eyes. She'd wanted him to kiss her. But did she want him more than she wanted to go home? And did he have a right to keep her here?

Damn, he wasn't ready to let her go yet! Not until he'd figured out this strange fascination he had with her. Not until he'd decided once and for all that she wasn't the type of woman he wanted. Not until he'd stopped craving the taste of her, stopped aching to touch her.

And not until he was able to fall asleep without her pretty face drifting through his mind and invading his dreams. No, he wouldn't tell her about the ride. If she wanted to leave him, then she'd have to find her own way back home from Key West. Until then, he had one more day to figure out just why he wanted her to stay.

"GET YOUR SHOES. We're going out."

Carrie looked up at Dev from her spot in the forward cockpit, where she'd stretched out with a magazine and a cool drink. He stood near the mast, still shirtless and dressed in the shorts he'd been in since his swim that morning. With every day that passed, he looked less like the businessman from Lake Grove and more like a beach bum.

She glanced around. "Out where? We're in the middle of nowhere."

"Then don't take your shoes," he said, jumping

down next to her. He grabbed her hand and pulled her to her feet. "You can go barefoot."

"But where are we going?"

"I've got something special I want to show you. We're taking the dinghy."

"But—"

He pressed his fingers to her lips and shook his head. "You wanted practice, didn't you? I want you to practice gracefully accepting my invitation. Then I want you to act like you're looking forward to spending time with me, that you're curious about my plans. Can you do that?"

Carrie nodded. "Yes, I suppose so."

Dev smiled, then dropped a quick kiss on her lips. "Very good. Lesson number one is going quite well, don't you think? You're a very good student, Carrie Reynolds."

Carrie smiled ruefully, then grabbed her shoes from the cockpit and followed him to the stern of the boat. She liked surprises, especially when they involved spending time with Dev. They'd spent most of the day together, sunning and swimming. Dev had shown her how to snorkel, and she found it as easy to float on her stomach as on her back— as long as Dev was holding on to her.

They saw a school of parrot fish and three different types of angelfish and an odd, four-eyed butterfly fish. Carrie was just getting comfortable with snorkeling, when Dev pointed out a school of small black sharks, each one barely longer than his arm. That put a quick end to her snorkeling adventures, as she quickly paddled back to the boat. A long nap was followed by a leisurely shower.

She'd taken special care with her hair and she'd

chosen the prettiest sundress she'd brought along. When she emerged from the hatchway, she had found Dev waiting for her at the dinner table, along with a wonderful meal of spicy crab cakes and Caesar salad. Carrie indulged in a margarita, made with fresh Key limes. After dinner, she settled into the cockpit to read, while Dev did a little more snorkeling off the bow of the boat. But she'd had a hard time concentrating on her magazine and, instead, occupied her time with watching Dev swim.

He was completely comfortable in the water, diving and surfacing as naturally as the porpoises they'd seen earlier that morning. But Carrie preferred Dev out of the water, where she could admire his lean, muscular body, the way droplets clung to the light dusting of hair on his chest and his impossibly long eyelashes, the way water streamed off his chest and down his belly when he pulled himself up on the boat.

As Dev leaned into the galley and retrieved a basket and blanket from Moira, Carrie couldn't help but admire his shoulders, so broad and well defined. Though she enjoyed the fact that Dev rarely wore any more than a pair of baggy shorts, she still couldn't help but wonder what he looked like without them. She'd found a certain pleasure in watching him dry off after his swims, and always managed to be close at hand with a fresh towel.

How strange that it had been just over a week ago when she'd admired his cashmere overcoat. Now she was fantasizing about Dev in the shower, Dev getting dressed in the morning, Dev naked between the sheets of her bed. She'd never been a connoisseur of the male anatomy, but she had to believe that Dev was just as incredible out of his clothes as he was in them. He probably had the cutest little rear—

"Ready?"

Carrie drew in a sharp breath and forced a smile, pushing aside her errant musings. "I'm ready," she said. "Where are we—" She paused. "Never mind. I don't care where we're going. I didn't mean to ask."

"That's the spirit," Dev teased, as he helped her down the ladder and into the dinghy. He untied the line and hopped into the back, then started the outboard. They slowly pulled away from *Serendipity* and headed out into the deeper channel. Tiny islands surrounded them, lush with mangrove, their roots tangled at the shore. In the late evening light, she could make out one of the bridges that connected the "mainland" Keys, one after the other, like the string in a necklace of pearls. The headlights of cars drifted up and over, then disappeared where the bridge met land.

The air was soft and warm, and Carrie could taste salt on the breeze as the dinghy skimmed across the water. A flock of seabirds wheeled overhead in the cloudless sky, diving and soaring as one. This truly was paradise. She found it hard to believe that the Keys they were seeing were the same as those packed with tourists. From the water, everything looked green and wild and perfectly deserted.

Dev had planned a wonderful vacation. Had Jillian come, she would have been witness to all this raw beauty. And she'd also have been the recipient of Dev's romantic attentions. But Carrie Reynolds was here instead, sharing his days and his nights, as if they actually meant something to each other. She glanced back at him, and he smiled. She should be happy for the time they did have together. After all, how many women got to live out their fantasies in such a wonderful setting?

Carrie stared out at the horizon and sighed. She hadn't lived out *all* her fantasies. At least not yet. There was one she'd been having that she liked to call her Robinson Crusoe fantasy.... She and Dev would visit a deserted island, much like the one they were approaching. And then, the outboard would break down, leaving them stranded. Of course, Fergus and Moira—or the Coast Guard— could come looking for them. Or as a last resort, Dev could probably swim back to *Serendipity* for help if he had to. And he might even be able to fix an outboard—but not in her fantasy.

Instead, they'd be completely alone. He would build a little house for them from palm fronds, and he'd catch fish and pick coconuts. And they'd spend all day together, swimming in a crystal clear lagoon and making love on the beach. They'd be wild and uninhibited, and they'd fall completely in love. And when they were rescued, there would be no doubt that they'd spend the rest of their lives together.

The dinghy jerked to a stop, the bow running up against the beach. Carrie watched as Dev hopped out and dragged the little boat up onto firmer sand. He held out his hand and helped her out.

"Are we here?" she asked.

He nodded. "This is it. Your very own deserted island. What do you think?"

She swallowed convulsively. Had he read her thoughts? Now all she needed to do was find some way to scuttle the outboard. "It's very...quiet."

"Exactly." He grabbed the blanket and basket and started down the beach. "Come on. The best spot's over here."

Carrie followed him, picking up her pace until she walked beside him. "How do you know about this place?"

"I came over here this afternoon while you were napping."

"What were you doing over here?"

"Just wait," he said, spreading the blanket out on the sand. "You'll see." He pulled her down next to him, then opened the basket and withdrew a bottle of wine and two glasses. When he'd filled her glass, he handed it to her, then raised his own. "To new friends," he murmured.

"New friends," she repeated. She touched his glass with hers, then took a sip of the wine.

They sat in silence on the sand, staring out at the horizon toward the sinking sun. Carrie wasn't sure what to say. Why had he brought her here? Had he enjoyed the same fantasy? "So," she finally said, turning toward him.

"So?"

"So why are we here?"

Dev took another sip of his wine. "Be patient. You'll see."

"We're just going to sit?"

"We could talk," Dev suggested. "That would

be good practice. Why don't you tell me about that cowboy of yours back in Helena?"

Carrie dropped her gaze to her wineglass. "Cowboy?"

"That guy you're in love with," Dev said.

"He's not a cowboy," Carrie explained in a soft voice. "He's—he's a businessman." She hesitated, not sure how far to go with the story. "I'm not sure what he makes or sells. But he's very good at it."

Dev paused for a long moment, then he gave her a sideways glance and smiled. "Sounds like a real catch. The kind of guy every woman wants. Rich, powerful, successful."

"That's not all a woman wants from a man," Carrie replied, angry that he'd think that of her. She wasn't some mercenary out to snag herself a rich husband!

Dev took her hand, deliberately lacing his fingers through hers. "Then why don't you tell me what women want, Carrie Reynolds? Enlighten me."

Grudgingly, she stifled her anger and answered his question as best she could. "I guess most women would like to find a good man. Someone kind and honest. And some women want children. A family and a happy life."

"And is that what you want, Carrie?"

She wrapped her arms around her knees and shrugged. "I think I'll know what I want when I find it. But until I find it, I'm not sure."

"But you're sure that you'll find it with this guy."

"Maybe. Or maybe with someone else." She felt his gaze on her, as if he'd touched her, and she turned to him. "What about you? What do you— What do *men* want?"

"Someone kind and honest," he said, recalling her own words. "Someone to love. Someone a lot like you."

Carrie felt a warm blush work its way up her cheeks. "You hardly know me," she said.

He grabbed her hand again and gave it a squeeze. "I know enough," he murmured. Dev drew a deep breath, then smiled. "There," he said, nodding toward the horizon. "That's why I brought you here."

Carrie turned to follow his gaze and her breath caught in her throat. The sky was on fire with orange and pink and lavender streaks. She'd never in her life seen a sunset so beautiful, so brilliant with color. Carrie turned back to Dev and found him staring at her. "It's perfect," she said. "I've never seen anything quite so lovely."

He nodded. "I thought you'd like it."

Carrie leaned over and pressed a kiss to his cheek. "Thank you for bringing me here. I won't forget it."

She turned back to watch the sun slowly sink over the Keys. They didn't say anything more to each other, just held hands and enjoyed the moment. And when the sun finally dipped below the horizon, Dev took them back to *Serendipity*, the dinghy cutting through the calm water under a deep blue sky specked with the first night stars.

They sat on deck for a long time, talking and laughing, until the moon had risen in the sky. When he made a move to turn in, Carrie expected him to share her bed again. But when she opened the door to her cabin, he stopped in the main saloon. She turned toward him and smiled. "It's all right."

Dev shook his head. "No. It's not."

"But you can sleep here. We did last night and there wasn't—I mean, we didn't—" She bit her bottom lip and waited for the hot flush in her cheeks to subside. "You're perfectly safe."

"There's nothing safe about sharing a bed with you, Carrie Reynolds," he murmured, pressing a gentle kiss to her forehead. "And don't ever think there is."

With that, he gently pushed her inside her cabin and pulled the door shut between them, leaving her alone. She sat down on the edge of the bed and rubbed her forehead where his lips had touched. A shiver worked its way up her spine, and she hugged herself and sighed.

There was nothing safe about sharing a bed with her? A tiny smile quirked the corners of her mouth. Did that mean she was dangerous? Carrie flopped back on the bed and pulled a pillow to her chest.

"Dangerous," she murmured. "Sharing a bed with me is dangerous." A giggle bubbled up in her throat. "I guess all this practice is starting to pay off."

6

DEV STOOD IN THE DOORWAY of Carrie's cabin, his shoulder braced against the bulkhead. She sat on the edge of her bed, unaware of his presence. This morning, she wore a pretty pink sundress that was cut tantalizingly low in the back. Her sunny blond hair tumbled over her shoulders in loose curls, and her arm was twisted behind her as she tried to apply the sunscreen between her shoulder blades. She turned toward him, and he watched as the soft fabric of her dress stretched tight against her breasts.

His fingers clenched as he remembered the feel of her beneath his palms, the lush warmth of her flesh, the tiny peaks of her nipples. He'd thought that she was Jillian that first night and had taken touching her for granted. Now he wished he could recall in more detail what it was like to caress her, to slide his hands along her naked hips.

He'd thought about that very thing for most of a sleepless night, swinging back and forth in that damn hammock. He could have followed Carrie through the door and crawled into bed with her. As she said, it was practical to share the only comfortable bed in the forward cabin. But he'd been tempted enough for one day.

Dev knew that if they shared a bed, he'd never

be able to keep his hands off her. Not after sharing that sunset. She had looked so beautiful in the last light of day, and he wanted to see her by first light. But he'd been all noble and chivalrous, retreating to his own tiny berth to cool his desire.

He'd never thought twice about taking a woman to his bed—until Carrie. But then, the women he'd slept with in the past had been more interested in a night of passion than in a future together. He'd made sure of that before he even took off his shoes. But Carrie wasn't made for one-night stands. She had a tender heart—and he didn't want to be responsible for breaking it. No, Carrie was the kind of woman that a man married, not the kind that a guy used and then tossed aside. The kind of woman that he *should* want to spend his life with— if he were interested in a happily-ever-after.

Dev stepped into her cabin and smiled. "Are you ready to go?"

She glanced up at him. "Ready? For what?"

"We're in Key West," he said, peering out the starboard porthole. "Home of Hemingway. I thought we could go out. You know, have a date— just for practice." Practice with Carrie was becoming a convenient reason to spend time with her.

Carrie squeezed another blob of sunscreen into her palm and gave him a nervous smile. "A date?"

"Yeah. We'll do the tourist thing, and then we can find a nice little restaurant. We can have dinner, and then maybe we can go dancing. All the things people do on a date."

"Dancing?" she repeated. She continued to struggle with the sunscreen, preoccupied with her own thoughts. "Did you know that Key West is the southernmost point in the United States? The continental United States, that is. Ka Lae, Hawaii, is much farther south."

"Did you read that in the guidebook?" Dev asked as he grabbed the bottle and squirted a good measure into his hand.

She shook her head. "I just knew it."

"And I suppose you know the northernmost point?"

"That's easy," she replied. "Point Barrow, Alaska, or West Quoddy Head, Maine." Her voice cracked slightly when he began to rub sunscreen over her shoulders, and a faint blush worked its way up her cheeks. "The—the highest point in the U.S. is Mount McKinley."

He smoothed the lotion across her back and shoulders. The instant he touched her, the warmth from her skin seeped into his bloodstream like a drug. He tried to focus on his task, but his mind drifted to the perfect curve of her shoulder, the silken skin at the base of her neck. His hands gentled to a soft caress, his fingers kneading and stroking, easing the tension he felt beneath them. "And the lowest point is Death Valley, right?"

"Umm," she said on a sigh. She closed her eyes and tipped her head to the side. "Two hundred eighty-two feet below sea level. The lowest point in the world is the Dead Sea. One thousand four feet lower than Death Valley."

Dev brushed her hair off her neck and applied the lotion to the skin below her jaw. "You know a lot about geography."

"I won a prize in high school," she said. "Four years in a row. It was my best subject."

Dev paused as he realized that this was another rare tidbit of information she'd volunteered about herself. He knew that she was from Helena, that she was in love with a man she'd never met, and that her father was a salesman of some sort and her mother had died when she was young. But that was all he knew about her past. He and Carrie had been existing entirely in the present.

"So you were one of those smart girls," Dev murmured. "But I bet you had lots of boyfriends."

Carrie's eyes opened and she glanced over her shoulder. "Oh, no. I never had a boyfriend in high school. I was really...shy. Not pretty at all. I had thick glasses and braces, and I was a little... chubby."

Dev skimmed his fingers along her shoulders, then rubbed the lotion into her upper arms, leaning closer in an effort to cover every bit of exposed skin. His gaze fixed at a spot at the base of her throat. He became mesmerized, watching her quickened pulse beat beneath her skin.

Instinct overcame common sense as Dev bent to touch his lips to the spot. He felt her stiffen beneath his hands, but then, as he traced a path to her shoulder, she relaxed and sighed softly. Time seemed to stand still, the outside world fading into nothing more than the soft slap of water on the side of the boat and the distant cry of a seagull.

His fingers slipped beneath the thin strap of her dress, and Dev pushed it aside. He heard her breath catch, and he waited for a moment, then slowly turned her to him, shifting on the bed until she sat between his thighs. He wanted to kiss her, to cover her mouth with his, to continue this tender seduction.

The true impact of his desire slowly sank into his mind. He'd never needed a woman quite the way he needed Carrie. Every fiber of his being had become twisted around her until she'd become an undeniable need, an ache that wouldn't subside.

He didn't want her to refuse, and took away her opportunity by bringing his mouth down on hers. A soft cry fluttered from her throat as their lips met—a sound that he wanted to believe was more desire than denial. As if to convince her, he deepened his kiss, tasting and teasing her tongue. The moment spun out around them, full of possibilities. But Dev held back, knowing full well that he should stop. "I would have asked you to the prom," he said against her mouth.

She stared up at him, the color high in her cheeks. "No, you wouldn't have. Men like you never notice women like me. You walk right by us on the street and never even give us a second glance."

Dev scowled and cupped her cheek in his hand. "What are you talking about? Of course I'd notice you."

Carrie blinked, then cleared her throat. "Maybe we should go." She jumped up and smoothed her dress. "Have you seen my hat? I shouldn't go out without my hat."

Dev groaned inwardly, confused by her behavior. "Hang on a second."

"I don't need any more sunscreen," she said as she searched for her hat. "You got every spot. I—I'm sure."

"That's not what I'm worried about." He reached for her hand, but she sidestepped him and rummaged through a pile of clothes on the chair. "Just sit down for a minute. I want to talk to you."

"We don't need to talk. We need to get going. Key West awaits!" she said with forced gaiety.

Dev finally caught her arm and drew her back to the bed, then pulled her down to sit beside him. "Do you realize that's the first time you've talked about yourself this whole trip? I want you to tell me more."

She stared down at her lap, where her fingers lay twisted together. "Why?"

"Because I want to know you, Carrie. Is there anything wrong with that?"

She considered his point for a long moment, then shrugged. "There's really no reason. I mean, after this vacation, we'll never see each other again. Why would you want to know more about me?"

Dev tipped her chin up, forcing her to meet his gaze. "Dammit, Carrie, I'm not asking you to reveal any national secrets here. I just want to know a little bit about you. We're friends, aren't we?"

"Are we?"

"Yes! I thought we agreed on that point."

Her gaze dropped to her hands again. "Friends don't kiss each other the way you just kissed me. And—and when you touch me, you don't touch me like you'd touch a friend."

Dev let out a long breath. She was right. At every turn, he'd taken advantage of her sweet nature and her naiveté, assuming her desire had been as strong as his. Maybe he'd just hoped that was so. But from the strained expression on her face, he could tell he'd been wrong. She hadn't wanted any of this. "I'm sorry," he said. "I didn't mean to push you."

"You didn't push me," she said. "I—I liked it when you kissed me. It was nice."

"Nice?"

Carrie nodded, smiling ruefully. "What woman wouldn't like the attention? I mean, you're handsome and charming—a real catch. And I'm sure all the women you've kissed have enjoyed it. And you kiss quite well."

"So, what's the problem then?"

Carrie sighed. "The problem is that in a few more days, we're both going to go home. And we'll never see each other again. I don't want to do something we might regret."

"Who says we'll never see each other again?" Dev snapped. His jaw tightened. He'd been the first person to assume that they'd never see each other again. But now, he wasn't so sure. He didn't want to think that Carrie would just disappear from his life without a trace. But what did that mean? Did he want a long-distance relationship with her? Or would the memories of their time together fade once he got back home?

"Come on, Dev," she said. "You have your life. It doesn't include me."

"And you have your cowboy, right?" Dev muttered.

"My cowboy?"

Jealousy niggled at his brain, but he pushed it aside. "That guy in Helena. The guy you're in love with."

A tiny smile twitched at her lips. "My businessman," she corrected.

"How do you know you love him?" Dev demanded. "I mean, how can you be sure? You barely know him, right? I knew Jillian for two years, and I thought I loved her. But I was wrong. I don't even think about her anymore—she barely crosses my mind. How can *you* be so sure?"

"I'm not sure of anything," she said, a hint of defensiveness creeping into her voice. "I have no idea what's going to happen when I get home. Maybe nothing. Or maybe my life will change completely. But one thing I do know is that this isn't real life. This is some kind of temporary paradise, where everything seems perfect." She stood up again and glanced around the room. "Now, where is my hat?"

"I know one thing, too," Dev said, pushing to his feet. "I'm real. I'm here with you, and he's not. That has to mean something, doesn't it?"

"It means that we can spend a lovely vacation together," Carrie said, turning to smile at him. "It means that we can walk around Key West and share the sights. We can be friends, Dev. That's all." She pulled back the rumpled covers at the foot of the bed and discovered her straw sunhat underneath. "Here it is. Now can we go?"

Grudgingly, Dev nodded. "All right, if this is what you want."

"It's what I want," Carrie said. With that, she pulled the hat down on her head and adjusted the brim low over her eyes. He couldn't see the truth there, but he had to believe what she said. Carrie

Reynolds wanted nothing more from him than friendship.

So why did that bother him? It certainly made his life simpler. He wouldn't have to worry about hurting her. She would never feel more for him than he felt for her. It was all perfectly platonic, Dev mused as he followed Carrie up on deck.

But if it was all so simple, then why was he so confused?

CARRIE SAT DOWN on a park bench and rubbed at her sore feet. She and Dev had managed to see most of the major sites in Key West in a single day, and had finally stopped at a pretty private garden filled with lush tropical plants. Above her head, a canopy of palms blocked the intense sun, casting her in cool shadow. Wispy ferns lined the pathways, and hanging orchids and vines tangled in strange trees called gumbo-limbos. The scent of green leaves and damp earth—like a perfume in the air—were so different from the salt breeze she'd become accustomed to.

She'd fallen in love with Key West, with its pretty Victorian homes and its bustling crowds, its noisy restaurants and narrow streets. The long-time natives, who called themselves Conchs, mingled freely with the tourists and vagabonds, creating a colorful group. Carrie and Dev had passed by the homes of Hemingway and Audubon on their walk. They'd visited museums dedicated to treasure hunters and wreckers—those 19th-century citizens who lured ships aground and then plundered them. And finally, they had climbed the stairs of a quaint white lighthouse and stared out over the town and the azure water beyond, searching the harbor for *Serendipity*.

A gentle breeze tugged at her skirt and tangled her hair, and she gazed down the path at Dev. He was intently studying an exotic flower, his head bent, his brow furrowed. She leaned back and sighed. All around her, colorful birds sang in a riotous chorus and insects buzzed, but all she could think about were the lies she'd told him earlier that morning.

If he'd just stop kissing her and touching her, she might be able to put their relationship in its proper place. But after their encounter in her cabin this morning, she wasn't quite sure what he wanted from her—or what she wanted from him. Though he claimed that he just wanted to be friends, every time she looked into his eyes, she saw something more.

And then there were all the things that *she* wanted—the needs that bubbled to the surface every time he came near. She'd wanted him to push her down on the bed, to tug at her dress and to press his mouth on her naked skin. In truth, she wanted him to ravish her.

She'd never thought much about sex before, but since that first night with Dev, she'd been completely preoccupied with the notion. If his kisses were any guide, sex with him would be beyond incredible.

So what was stopping her? That's what she'd come on this vacation for, wasn't it? To collect a little experience. If she set her mind to it, she was certain that she could lure Dev into her bed again, and this time to do more than just sleep.

Carrie sighed. "Don't be ridiculous," she murmured to herself. "You've never seduced a man in your life." Besides, seducing Dev would not be like seducing some stranger at a singles resort. With Dev, her heart was at risk. She'd fallen in love with him without ever talking to him. How could she possibly fall *out* of love with him after sharing such a profound intimacy? Making love to Dev Riley would be the worst mistake of her life.

She watched him walk toward her, admiring his loose-limbed gait, his narrow hips and his muscular legs. Though she'd made her feelings quite clear, Carrie had expected him to test her again, to kiss her or to touch her sometime during their tour around Key West. But the closest he came was holding her hand as they strolled the streets. If he had any lusty thoughts, he'd hidden them quite well. And as the afternoon was waning, she'd convinced herself that their encounter had been so forgettable that it had slipped from his mind the moment after it happened.

"Are you ready for dinner?" Dev asked as he stood in front of her.

Carrie nodded, her eyes slowly drifting up his body. "It's beautiful here. Hard to believe we're still in the U.S. Everything is so…exotic."

Dev chuckled. "If the Conchs had had their way back in 1982, we wouldn't be in the U.S.," he said, grabbing her hand and pulling her up. "The Border Patrol set up roadblocks on the highway and tried to catch drug runners, but they only made the locals mad. So the citizens staged a mock secession and the Border Patrol backed off."

"Did you read that in the guidebook?" she teased.

He pulled her up to stand in front of him. "No," Dev said, acting insulted. "I read it on a sign outside the tourist center."

She slipped her arm through his. "I'm glad I got the wrong vacation," she said as they strolled down the pathway. "I can't think of any other place I'd rather be right now. Tomorrow, maybe we can see the aquarium."

"We're going to Cristabel Key tomorrow morning," Dev said. "It' going to be the nicest stop on the trip."

She sighed. "I keep thinking that I've just seen the most interesting place, and then the next day is better. I should go on vacation more often."

"And where would you go next?" he asked.

Carrie shrugged. "I don't know. It would have to be someplace warm. In Chicago, everything is so gray and depressing. Here, it's so warm and green."

"Chicago is cold," Dev agreed. "But not colder than Helena, is it?"

She turned and looked at him, confusion muddling her brain. What had she just said? Had she mentioned Chicago? "Oh, yes," she finally replied. "Helena is much colder. I don't want to go back to Helena. *Helena* is definitely cold and gray."

"We could stay," Dev suggested. "We could quit our jobs and get ourselves a little hut on the beach. I could pick coconuts, and you could sell shells on the street corner."

Carrie giggled, relieved that she'd covered her little mistake. "You'd be so bored," she continued.

"You love your work. I mean, you never take time off and this is the first—" She stopped short. What was she saying now? If she didn't know Dev, how could she possibly know these things? Unless, of course, Susie had told her—which she had. "I mean, you do love your work, don't you?"

He gave her another odd look and shrugged. "Of course I do. But until I took this vacation, I didn't realize what I'd been missing. I need to take more time off."

"There are so many interesting places to visit," she murmured, afraid to say anything else. All this easy conversation had caused her to lower her guard. If she wasn't careful, she'd say something that would give her away!

He squeezed her hand. "To tell you the truth, I'd rather be here with you than anyplace else in the world."

Carrie smiled. "That's very sweet," she said. When he didn't reply, she looked over at him and found him staring at her.

"I came on this trip wanting to get away from women. After Jillian, I'd decided to write off the entire sex. But then you turned up in my bed and everything changed. That guy you love is a lucky man, Carrie."

"He doesn't know how lucky," she murmured, turning her gaze back to the path in front of her.

But would Dev really feel lucky if he knew that *he* was the object of her desire, that *he* was the man she was "practicing" for? Or would he feel betrayed by her lies, tricked by her deceptions? Carrie drew in a long breath. She'd just have to make sure that he never found out.

CARRIE TIPPED HER FACE UP to the starlit sky and spun around in a circle. The effects of too much rum made her legs a bit wobbly, and Dev caught her in his arms and steadied her. She was warm and flushed, and her lips were so tempting that he had to fight the impulse to kiss her again. With a giggle, she grabbed his hand and twirled beneath his arm in a fancy two-step that she'd learned just that night.

"I've never danced like that before," she said.

Dev chuckled and tugged her into his arms, swaying with the twangy country ballad that drifted out of Captain Billy's waterfront tavern. Her body was warm, her breasts soft against his chest, her waist circled by his arm. "And how have you danced?"

"By myself," Carrie replied. "In my pajamas with my cat. Eloise loves Madonna. But I'm partial to Motown. We've danced away many a Saturday night together."

Dev smiled and closed his eyes, inhaling the sweet scent of her hair. Not many women would admit to such a lackluster social life. The women he knew preferred to create an image of sophistication and power, completely indifferent to those who didn't share their stunning selection of male suitors. He'd always felt like the latest on a long list. But with Carrie, there was no one waiting in the wings—except her cowboy from Helena.

Dev slipped his arm around her shoulders, and they began to walk toward the marina. It was nearly midnight and Key West was just coming alive. Tourists and townsfolk had gathered to party away the night, sipping rum concoctions that raised the level of merriment with each little umbrella tossed aside. As they strolled past taverns and clubs, a crazy cacophony of music drifted out onto the street: country, rhythm and blues, reggae and a lot of Jimmy Buffett.

They'd begun the evening with dinner at a small café that specialized in Caribbean cuisine. While Dev wasn't as adventurous as Carrie in his choices, they both sampled each other's selections while they carried on an easy conversation. With each glass of wine, Carrie relaxed a bit more. Though she was always careful about what she revealed, she talked about everything from her childhood to her favorite flavor of ice cream: rum raisin.

By the time she had polished off her crème brûlée, Dev had decided that she was possibly the most beautiful woman in the world—not in the accepted sense of the world, but in a way he'd come to value more than a polished appearance and a perfect body. She radiated beauty from within, her sweet nature and sunny outlook lighting up the room around them.

And she was also the most mysterious and intriguing woman he'd known. At times, she was completely open, answering his questions without hesitation. And at other points in their conversation, he could sense a barrier between them, as if she were evaluating what she was about to say, editing it for his consumption. He could only believe that she wanted to hold a part of herself from him, protecting her vulnerability.

She'd asked him about his business, and he'd bored her with all the details. He usually glossed over his childhood with few words, but he told

Carrie about it all. About living in a series of run-down apartments with parents who were forced to work two jobs each to support five children. About his father who'd scrimped and saved from his factory job to open his own electronics business. About how Dev had helped him turn that business into a multinational corporation before he retired to enjoy a life that had once been so hard.

They'd moved on from dinner to Captain Billy's, a rowdy bar with a bartender—Billy himself—who claimed a colorful background as a smuggler, gambler and all-around rogue. Billy talked Carrie into trying a Buccaneer's Delight, a wicked blend of rum and tropical fruit juice. It was served with two straws in a bowl shaped like a pirate ship, and by the time she lowered the level to the poop deck, she'd accepted Dev's invitation to dance.

"Where are we going next?" Carrie asked.

"Back to *Serendipity*. It's time to put you to bed. Captain Fergus wants to leave for Cristabel Key in a few hours."

"But I don't want to leave Key West," she said. "I like it here. Nobody cares who you are or where you come from. I can just be me."

"You'll like Cristabel Key," Dev said. "I promise."

"But there's so much more to do here. Why don't we stay here until we have to go home?"

Dev hadn't bothered to tell Carrie about the last stop on their trip. And she hadn't questioned Captain Fergus about their itinerary. He wasn't sure she'd approve of Cristabel Key, and he didn't want to take the chance that she wouldn't. He wasn't sure why he was so determined to take her there.

The private villa on Cristabel Key was supposed to be the most beautiful and romantic spot in all of the Keys, and he'd chosen it for one purpose—as the spot where he'd propose to Jillian.

But now, Jillian was out of his life. He wanted to share his last two days of vacation with Carrie— alone on their very own private island. Dev wasn't sure what he expected to happen on Cristabel Key. Did he hope that he'd suddenly understand his feelings for Carrie? Or did he want to put a pleasant end to their brief relationship before he went back home? Maybe deep down he was hoping that he and Carrie would figure it out between them.

But what then? With Jillian, he'd at least had a plan. And Dev was the kind of guy who always liked to have his strategy mapped out ahead of time. But Carrie wasn't some business objective that he could achieve. She was a mass of contradictions wrapped up in a body that drove him mad with desire. She was in love with another man, yet every time he kissed her, he felt her soften in his arms. And she had invited him into her bed, chaste as the experience had been.

So why was he so afraid to take a chance? Why not see just where a little passion might lead? He'd decided to be honorable when it came to Carrie, but Dev was beginning to believe that he was using honor as an excuse to avoid his real feelings.

If he didn't make love to Carrie, then he couldn't possibly fall in love with her. And she couldn't fall in love with him. And if they didn't love each other, then he'd have no problems leaving her. So that was that—no more kissing, no more desire, no thoughts of ripping her clothes off and making love to her until neither of them could think.

Serendipity bobbed gently against the pier as they approached. Dev held on to Carrie's hand, pulling her away from the edge of the dock when she came too close. She'd had a little too much rum that night, and would no doubt sleep well. When they reached the boat, he helped her on board and then down the steps into the main saloon.

"We need music," Carrie said, slipping her arms around his neck as if she'd done the same a million times before. "I want to dance."

Dev smiled and kissed her on the tip of her nose. "And I think you should sleep, Carrie."

She closed her eyes and swayed slightly, a smile touching her perfect mouth. "Maybe you're right."

"I am right," he said, his gaze fixed on her lips. Just one small kiss couldn't hurt. A good-night kiss between friends. He bent over her and covered her mouth with his.

But once she opened beneath him, all his resolve drained from his body and his mind focused on the taste and feel of her. She moaned softly, and he deepened his kiss, cupping her cheeks in his hands.

Carrie drew back and looked up at him, her eyes wide. "I thought we decided we weren't going to do that anymore."

"I can't help it, Carrie," he murmured. "Sometimes I just have to kiss you." He traced her mouth with his thumb. "How about if every time the urge strikes, I just ask? Would that be all right?"

"I'll say no," she warned, a pretty blush staining her cheeks.

He furrowed his hand through the hair at her nape and tugged her head back. His eyes bore into hers, and he watched the glint of humor slowly fade. "Can I kiss you again, Carrie?"

"No," she murmured.

He brushed his lips over hers. "All right, then this is the last time."

"The last time," she repeated.

He kissed her again, his tongue teasing hers, probing until she returned his desire in full measure. His hands slid along her rib cage, spanning her waist, then moving up to brush her breasts. But he stopped, suddenly aware of what he was about to do. A kiss was a kiss, but he'd been about to cross the threshold into something much more intimate.

Dev drew back and waited until she opened her eyes, hoping to read her reaction. She blinked, and he watched as the aftereffects of their kiss slowly faded from her eyes, only to be replaced by undisguised…pleasure. "That was—nice," she said in a hesitant voice. She swallowed hard and forced a smile. "Thank you."

"You don't have to thank me," Dev said.

"It was very good…practice."

"Practice?" he asked.

Carrie nodded. "Yes. Our date. The—the kissing. It was just for practice, wasn't it?"

Dev ground his teeth. Why did she deny the passion she felt? He saw it so clearly in her eyes, and she knew damn well why he'd kissed her. "I think we've had enough for one night." He grabbed her shoulders and steered her toward her cabin.

"Practice makes perfect," she said softly.

Actually, practice didn't make perfect. As far as

Dev was concerned, Carrie was already perfect. The way she grew pliant in his arms, the way she opened so eagerly to his kiss—that was perfection. It was as if they were destined to be together, against all common sense, his need growing more intense with every passing hour, instead of subsiding with time.

But time was one thing they didn't have. In two days she'd go back to Montana, back to the man she loved. And he'd go back to his life in Chicago. Their vacation together would end...and real life would begin again.

She glanced back at him. "Do you want to sleep with me tonight?" she asked.

Dev stopped short. "What?"

"In my bed. That hammock can't be comfortable. I don't mind. I know you'll be a perfect gentleman."

"The hell I will," he muttered beneath his breath. He was growing a little tired of playing the gentleman with Carrie—especially when she responded so eagerly to his every touch, yet denied her response! There had to be a way to make her face her passion. To make her want him as much as he wanted her.

Dev was accustomed to getting what he wanted, and he wanted Carrie. But he hadn't a clue how to go about getting her. And once he had her, what did he really want—one night of great sex, or many nights spent staring into her eyes and listening to her voice? Until he knew exactly what he wanted, it would probably be best to stay out of her bed.

He forced a smile, then turned and opened the door to his own tiny berth. "Good night, Carrie. Sleep well."

7

"WE'RE ALONE? Completely alone?" Carrie stood in the middle of the airy foyer, her luggage scattered around her feet. Her voice echoed from the cool Spanish tile floors up to the top of the staircase. She turned to Dev and frowned. "What about Fergus and Moira, and the rest of the guests?"

"Fergus and Moira are gone," he said. "And there are no other guests."

Carrie pushed her luggage aside and raced to the front doors. The view of the ocean was expansive, and she could see *Serendipity* slowly receding from the dock, skimming through calm water in the direction of Key West. "I don't understand. Why would they leave us?"

"A private island isn't very private when there's a crowd around," Dev murmured from over her shoulder. "Look at that beach. Isn't that beautiful? And can you believe this house?"

"There must be servants," she said, a hint of desperation creeping into her voice. "Where are the servants?"

"I asked that they come only in the morning. All our meals have been prepared. The refrigerator is stocked. We have everything we need right here. And if there's an emergency, there's a radio phone."

Carrie bit back a frustrated oath. "Why didn't you tell me we were going to be here alone?" she demanded.

"I didn't think it would make a difference," Dev replied with a shrug. "We've essentially been alone this entire vacation. We've slept in the same bed on more than one occasion. What's so different about this?"

Carrie scowled, then spun on her heel and gathered up her luggage. "It's different," she muttered. *Way different,* she thought to herself. On *Serendipity,* they had chaperones, boundaries, agreements. Here they had...the most romantic setting she could ever imagine. The villa looked like something out of a movie or *Lifestyles of the Rich and Famous,* it was so perfect.

The white stucco home was built just yards from the beach with a wide covered verandah spanning one entire side on both floors. The design combined Spanish and French influences with some elements of the Conch architecture that she'd seen in Key West. Ceilings were high and decorated with softly whirring fans. Sheer curtains billowed around shuttered French doors. The interior was decorated in soothing colors of salmon and cream, and potted palms rustled in the ocean breeze that filled the house. The atmosphere was peaceful and exotic—and very disconcerting.

"You're not angry, are you?" he asked.

"We had an agreement," she said as she struggled up the stairs with her luggage. "Don't you remember?"

Dev followed hard on her heels, and she stumbled twice before he grabbed the largest of her bags and hauled it to the top of the stairs. He stood in front of her, blocking her way. "What agreement?"

"You're supposed to ask first," she said. "And if I want to say no, I can!"

"That's the kissing agreement. What does that have to do with this place?"

"Oh, don't play dumb," Carrie said, stepping around him. She strode down the hall and turned into the first bedroom. A huge mahogany four-poster bed dominated the room, with yards and yards of mosquito netting draped over it. She groaned. "Look at this! You planned all this. You brought me here to—to seduce me!"

Dev laughed out loud. "Actually, my travel agent planned all this a couple of weeks ago. And I planned to ask Jillian to marry me here. This was going to be the spot where I proposed." He glanced around the hallway, then pointed to the large bed. "That would probably have been the exact spot, if you must know."

Carrie felt the heat in her cheeks rise, right along with her mortification. Oh, Lord! What had she been thinking? How could she have forgotten Jillian? Dev hadn't brought her here on purpose. This had just been part of his original itinerary—a part bought and paid for, a part that had never included her.

She chastised herself in silence. Leave it to Susie to find a place like this for him. Her partner was a top-notch travel agent—after all, not every agent could find accommodations so luxurious. The villa reeked of romance, was positively perfect for seduction, and had every amenity a guest could desire. And it was the last place in the world she wanted to be with Dev Riley.

"I'm sorry," she said. "I jumped to the wrong conclusion. I just thought—"

Dev covered her lips with his finger in a gesture that had become so familiar. Why couldn't she just think before she spoke? Why did she have to blurt out the first thing that came into her head?

"Well, you thought right," he admitted. "Maybe I deliberately neglected to tell you that we'd be alone here. Maybe I did bring you here to seduce you. I'm not really sure myself. But I do know that I wanted to spend our last days of vacation here, with you. What's wrong with that?"

Carrie opened her mouth to protest, but he stopped her words again, this time with a quick kiss—so brief and fleeting and incredibly intoxicating.

"And you're also right about our agreement," he said.

"Our agreement?"

"The kissing agreement. It's also valid for other...pleasures. Nothing will happen here, Carrie, unless you want it to. Understand?"

She nodded, then forced a smile. Unless she *wanted* it to? That's all she'd been thinking about from the moment she'd found him in her bed! She'd weighed all the pros and cons and changed her mind a million times, and she still wasn't sure what she wanted. But now she knew that if she wanted her ultimate fantasy to come true, she'd have to ask for it!

How did one go about asking to be seduced? She'd always thought that it was an unspoken kind of thing. Something that both parties just sensed when the time was right. And when was she supposed to ask? Over dinner? Before retiring for the night? Oh, what difference did it make anyway? Carrie knew that she could never work up the courage to make such a request.

"So, is this bed yours or mine?"

She glanced over her shoulder at Dev. "What?"

"This place has five bedrooms," he said. "Is this the one you want?"

Carrie nodded. With that, Dev grabbed her luggage and stepped around her. She watched him set the bags on the bed, then walk over to the French doors and throw them open to the breeze. His dark hair fluttered as he looked out at the ocean. She imagined him in that exact spot, late at night, staring at the water, while she lay curled up in that magnificent bed. His skin would be slick with sweat and his eyes hooded with exhaustion. And she'd want him all over again.

Her throat tightened. Would that scene come to life before this vacation was over? Or was it just a silly flight of fancy to believe that this room might be the place where they would make love? If she wanted it to happen, it would have to happen soon. They only had two nights on this island before their vacation was over.

Carrie's heart twisted in her chest as she thought about leaving Dev. It wasn't as if she'd never see him again. He'd still wander into her life every now and then, when he came into the agency. But it wouldn't be the same. He wouldn't know who she was, or even that she was near. But she would be there, watching him and thinking about everything they'd shared, taking secret pleasure in the memories.

"I'm going to hit the beach," Dev said. "Want to come?"

Carrie shook her head. "No, I think I'll unpack and explore the house. You go ahead. Have fun."

Dev nodded, then walked out of the room, leaving her alone. She crossed over to the French doors and stepped out onto the terrace, then drew a long breath of the salt air. Maybe she should stop worrying about what *might* or *could* happen—and just have a pleasant time.

She returned to the bed and threw open her suitcase. Shopping in Key West had been a grand success. She'd bought a beautiful dress made of gauzy fabric. The flowing skirt and tight bodice made her feel so feminine, and the pale color set off the bit of tan she'd managed to acquire over the past week. She'd wear it to dinner tonight. And she'd bought some earrings made of hammered silver and polished rose quartz that dangled provocatively against her neck.

Carrie pulled out another bag, then dumped its contents on the bed. A riot of color spilled out in front of her: electric blue, sunny yellow, bright fuchsia. The swimsuit and matching *pareu* had been an impulse buy. She'd realized that she couldn't continue swimming in her nightgown, and there would probably be an opportunity to swim with Dev again before the week was over. She wanted to be prepared.

Carrie had never ventured inside a swimsuit, probably because she didn't have a very high opinion of her thighs. "Maybe it's time I took a chance," she murmured as she kicked off her shoes. Her sundress slipped down around her feet as she stepped out of it. Carrie held the suit up to her body. She hadn't had the nerve to try it on in the store; she'd just bought it in the same size that she wore in dresses.

Drawing a deep breath, she stripped off her bra and panties, then stepped into the swimsuit. In all of life's experiences, nothing could terrify a woman more than trying on a swimsuit, she mused—except maybe looking in the mirror afterward. She snatched up the sheer *pareu* and tied it around her waist, then hesitantly walked to the bathroom that adjoined her bedroom.

She found a full-length mirror on the back of the bathroom door, but for a long moment, she was afraid to open her eyes. ''If it looks horrible, you can take it off,'' she said to herself. ''If it's really awful, you can throw it away.'' But when she let her gaze drift down the length of her body, she was pleasantly surprised.

As a terminally single woman without prospects, she'd never spent much time looking at her body in the mirror. In fact, she usually avoided mirrors. But maybe she'd been wrong. With her new hair color and her sun-kissed skin, she looked pretty good in a bathing suit.

''All right,'' Carrie said, straightening her shoulders. ''I put it on. Now the next step is going out in public.'' Actually, being in public would probably be a far sight easier than walking out on that private beach with only Dev Riley to see her. She hurried from the bathroom and looked out the French doors. She saw Dev on the beach below, wading through the surf.

"What's the worst that could happen?" she asked herself. Carrie fiddled with the knot on her *pareu*. "He could laugh. He could mistake me for a beached whale or a Russian submarine." But over the past week, Dev had seen her at her very worst—seasick and sunburned and sulky. Maybe it was time for him to see her as a real woman—a sexy woman. A woman he might want to seduce.

She ran her fingers through her hair and pasted a smile on her face. "Go for it," she said. "The only thing you have to fear is fear itself...and utter humiliation and total embarrassment." But then, she'd already faced both many times on this trip.

As she strolled down the terrace stairs and out onto the beach, she tried to concentrate on proper posture, attempting to walk casually. But her knees were wobbly and her pulse was pounding and she could barely draw a breath for trying to hold in her stomach.

Dev had wandered down along the water and now sat in the sand, staring out at the horizon. She waited for him to notice her, but he seemed to be lost in his own thoughts. Carrie was nearly upon him, when he turned in her direction. Her heart skipped as she saw the look of appreciation in his eyes and the slow smile that curled his lips.

"Wow," he said, his gaze drifting down along her body.

Carrie smiled and took another step toward him. But he suddenly scrambled to his feet and held out his hand.

"Carrie, watch out for that—"

A vicious stinging sensation shot through her foot and up her leg, and she cried out. Dev was at her side in an instant. He scooped her up in his arms as she moaned in agony. A million needles of pain snaked up her limb and made her head swim. Tears came to her eyes. "What happened?" she asked.

"You stepped on a jellyfish," Dev said. "God, Carrie, you're a walking disaster."

She groaned and buried her head against his shoulder. "I knew I shouldn't have put this damn swimming suit on. I should have stayed in my room and taken a nap."

Dev chuckled and nuzzled her neck. "And miss that entrance? Not a chance."

"HOW'S THE FOOT?"

Carrie looked up from her bed to find Dev standing in the doorway of her room. He had a tray in his arms. "It still hurts," she said, wincing at the pain. "But I think I'll be all right. Thanks to you."

He had an uncanny knack for saving her when she found herself in distress. Dev had carried her all the way from the beach to the house, as if she weighed less than air. And then he'd retrieved a bottle of ammonia from the kitchen and dabbed a bit on her foot. Almost immediately, the pain had subsided, but he had insisted on using the radio phone to call a doctor. When the doctor had pronounced his treatment adequate, Dev had finally relaxed enough to tease her about her bad luck.

"I brought you something to eat," he said as he approached the bed. "I figured you might not be in any shape to walk to the kitchen."

Carrie pushed up in the bed, and Dev adjusted the pillow behind her back. "Why do I always seem to be at my worst when I'm with you?"

He placed the tray on the bedside table and sat down beside her. "How can you say that? I find your little exploits very entertaining. My vacation would have been boring without you."

"And here I was trying to be sexy," Carrie muttered.

He glanced down at her, an eyebrow raised in surprise. "Really?"

She forced a lighthearted giggle and tried to cover her comment. "No. Not deliberately. I mean, I wasn't trying to—you know."

"Of course not," he said in a tight voice. For a moment, she thought he was angry with her, but then returned her smile, his gaze skimming her face. He took her hand and laced his fingers through hers, rubbing his thumb against her palm in a gentle massage.

Carrie risked a look up at him and found him staring at her with an enigmatic expression. Why not admit that she was hoping to catch his eye? Even better, why not just come right out and ask him to spend the night in her bed? How hard could it be? Not any harder than parading down a beach in a swimming suit for the first time in her life. Carrie marshaled all her resolve, ignored all her fears, summoned every bit of her courage and opened her mouth—but she couldn't do it.

After a long moment, he sighed, then stood up. "I'll let you get some rest now. I'm going to go for a swim before bed." He walked to the door. "Sleep well, Carrie. If you need anything—anything at all—just call me."

She wanted to call out to him that very moment, to ask him to stay, to tell him that she needed his lips on her neck, his hands on her body. But instead she leaned back into the down pillows, quelling the impulse. Maybe if she just relaxed and closed her eyes, she'd wake up in the morning completely refreshed and totally convinced that she really didn't want Dev Riley as much as she thought she did.

CARRIE WASN'T SURE how long she'd slept, or if she'd slept at all. Her foot ached and her leg had grown stiff from lying elevated on a pillow. She pushed up on her elbows and plucked at the damp fabric of her nightgown. The ocean breeze had stilled, and the room had grown quiet and close. She reached over and turned off the lamp, but the moonlight streaming through the windows was enough to illuminate her surroundings and keep her awake.

With a resigned sigh, she swung her legs off the bed and gingerly tried to walk. To her surprise, she was able to bear almost all her weight on her sore foot. She walked over to the French doors, hoping to catch a bit of a breeze to cool her skin. But the sight that met her eyes took her breath away, and made her heart lurch.

Dev stood on the sand, facing the ocean, the moonlight silhouetting his body. He no longer wore the shorts she'd seen him in earlier. He had discarded them and was now completely naked. Her gaze took in his broad back, his narrow waist, his long, muscular legs. Holding her breath, she slowly stepped out onto the terrace, grateful for the shadows cast by the stucco pillars.

Unaware of her, he slowly walked into the water up to his waist, then dropped down until he submerged. Carrie bit her lip and waited for him to appear again, and when he did, his body gleamed wet in the silver light. He looked like an ancient god sprung from the sea, fierce and untamed, stroking powerfully through the water, then diving beneath the surface.

Carrie watched him swim for a long time, wondering at the energy that he found. Perhaps he was as restless as she was. Maybe he was even thinking about her, contemplating what might happen between them if they shared a bed one last time. She moaned softly and turned away from the scene, leaning back against the cool pillar, trying to still her hammering heart.

But when she went to watch him again, she saw him striding up the beach, still naked, a towel hung around his neck. Carrie found herself transfixed, frozen in that spot at the top of the terrace stairs and unable to retreat. Dev looked up and saw her there, then stopped. For a long time, they just watched each other, their gazes locked, unwavering, unfettered desire burning a pathway between them.

"I—I want you to ask me," she said, her voice trembling. She gulped back her nerves. "Please."

Slowly, he slipped the towel from his shoulders and hitched it around his waist, regarding her with a wary eye. His hand gripped the railing as he ascended the stairs. "What do you want me to ask, Carrie?"

Carrie shook her head. "Don't make this difficult, because if you do I'm going to change my mind."

He nodded, approaching with silent steps, his bare feet quiet on the tile. His hand found her cheek and he gently caressed her face, tipping her gaze up to his. "I want you, Carrie. Do you want me?"

"I want you," she said, her hands splaying across his damp chest.

He sucked in his breath and tipped his head back, and she snatched her hands away, afraid that she'd made a mistake. But without looking at her, he captured her fingers again and put them back where they'd been. "You can touch me," he said. "I love the feel of your hands on my body."

She'd never been so bold with a man, but she needed to know him, to explore his body until it became familiar to her fingers and burned in her memory—the sharp angles of his shoulders, the rippled muscles of his belly, the soft line of hair that ran from his collarbone to beneath the towel. Every place she touched was hard and smooth, as if carved from marble.

Carrie had never felt such an overpowering need before. There had been other men in her life, but no one had ever possessed her soul like Dev Riley. He had begun as a fantasy and now he stood before her, so real and so alive. All the trepidation she should have felt had dissolved, and now she was fixed on her purpose—to love him fully and completely, to share every intimacy.

"I'm not very good at this," she murmured.

Dev bent closer, the warmth from his body seeping into hers. "You're doing just fine. Don't be afraid of me, Carrie. I promise, I won't hurt you." He drew her into his arms and molded her body to his, and she pressed closer until she could feel the hard ridge of his desire beneath the towel.

"Please, don't make me do this alone," she murmured. "Touch me."

It was as if he'd conceded all the power to her, and now she'd given it back to him, willingly and eagerly. When his hands skimmed her shoulders, brushing aside the straps of her nightgown, she shivered. Slowly, he pushed the soft fabric down along her arms, revealing her breasts to his touch.

Dev traced a line of kisses from her collarbone to her nipples, branding her skin. When his lips touched the hard nubs, electric shocks of desire pulsed through her body and she bit back a moan. For a moment, she thought her knees might buckle, but he clasped her waist between firm hands and held on tightly. Nothing before had ever felt so right, so perfect.

She'd held on to her passion so tightly, and for so long, that releasing all her inhibitions felt like soaring, rising and falling on currents of warm salt air like a seabird in flight. Carrie let herself drift, as Dev carefully peeled off her nightgown, caressing every inch of skin along the way, kneading and massaging her flesh. When she was completely naked, he stood and pulled off his towel.

Her breath caught in her throat at the sight of him fully aroused. She reached out to touch him, then pulled her hand back. Dev smiled and nuzzled her neck. "Come with me," he said, taking her hand.

He led her back down to the beach and into the water. Carrie expected the ocean to be cold, but a delicious warmth rose over her body as she walked in. Dev held on to her waist and tipped her back until her hair swirled around her head. The waves tossed them gently in the surf. She arched her back, and he drew his hand from the base of her throat to her belly, sliding frictionless over her slippery skin.

Every sensation was heightened by the water as their hands deliberately searched, their bodies pressed against each other. Dev hitched her knees up on his hips, and she felt him brush against her, hard and unyielding. She held her breath, wondering if he'd take her here, in the water. But instead, he carried her to the beach and gently laid her on a blanket.

Once again, his mouth played havoc with her body. Every nerve tingled at the touch of his tongue, and when his fingers found her core, she moaned out loud. Carrie raked her hands through his damp hair and pulled him closer. But when he moved lower to taste her, she let him go, sliding along with the languid passion that his touch evoked.

His mouth was sweet torment, teasing her until a knot of passion tightened within her. Carrie's mind screamed for release and her nerves hummed. All she could feel was him, between her legs. Slowly, he brought her closer, then drew away, taunting her with his power. But then, the warmth twisted inside her and she knew she'd break this time, rather than bend. Carrie urged him on with incoherent words, murmuring his name over and over until it matched the rhythm of her pulse.

The tension was exquisite and she cried out for her release. And then a wave broke on the shore, washing over her, drowning her, stealing her breath from her body. Nothing had ever prepared her for the power of her pleasure, the sheer awe of her need for him. As the shudders and shivers subsided, she pulled him up until he covered the length of her, warm and heavy.

With tantalizing patience, he slipped inside her. She watched his face as he moved, taking pleasure in the expression that suffused his handsome features. Hard and assured, he began to love her, first with great gentleness and then with a rising passion that threatened to carry them both over the edge, never to return.

He murmured her name once as he neared his peak, his body tensing above her. His breath was soft and warm against her ear as urgent sounds of passion slipped from his lips. And then, one smooth stroke and he was there, exploding inside her.

She'd never known anything that came close to what they'd shared, the effect that it had on both her body and soul. She loved this man, more than she'd ever imagined. Her silly infatuation had transformed into a deep, soul-shattering realization. She wanted him in her body, in her future, in her life. Forever.

They made love again on the beach, wrapped snugly in the blanket, and she fell asleep in his arms. Carrie barely remembered him carrying her back up to her bedroom, barely noticed when he slipped into bed beside her and cradled her body against his. But when she woke up to his touch, she welcomed the feel of him on top of her, his hips nestled between her legs, the sweet sensation of him entering her again so slowly, and she knew that all her dreams had come true.

As he brought her to another climax, she realized that she'd found paradise in his arms. And as for reality—she'd leave that to the light of day.

HE WOKE UP ALONE, but as Dev rolled over in bed, he had to smile. Carrie couldn't have gone far. They were on an island with no way off. If he waited long enough, she'd come back to bed, and they could continue with all the pleasures they'd enjoyed the night before.

They'd finally fallen asleep in each other's arms in the very early morning, as the sky was beginning to turn from black to dark blue, and the birds were starting their morning songs. He'd wanted to watch the sunrise with her, but they'd both been too exhausted and had slept through it. No matter, though—they'd have the sunrise tomorrow morning.

He stared at the ceiling and let out a long breath. Why did the thought of tomorrow wrench his gut? Dev still wasn't sure how they'd part, what he'd say, where he'd leave everything. He'd considered all his options; he'd even considered asking her to move to Chicago so they might find out if their relationship had a future. But his experience with Jillian made him leery of commitment.

Did he love Carrie Reynolds? For the moment, he did. His feelings for Carrie had grown way beyond what he'd ever felt for Jillian, and in only a short week together. But he was loathe to trust those feelings. He wasn't sure that they'd last outside the bedroom—or outside this paradise they'd found. He'd always heard vacation affairs were like a flash fire—hot and intense, but short-lived.

Dev rolled onto his side, then sat up and stretched his arms over his head. He planned to enjoy Carrie as long as he could. As for their future, he'd deal with that problem when it came up. He tugged on a pair of shorts and headed to the door. Right now, he needed coffee—and Carrie, not necessarily in that order.

The house was quiet as he left the bedroom, the only sound coming from the waves that rushed against the shore. The Spanish tiles were cool on his bare feet and a fresh breeze blew through the French doors. Dev slowly walked down the stairs, rubbing his eyes and yawning.

Maybe she'd gone looking for breakfast. The housekeeper would have arrived by now and probably had already started the coffee. But when Dev reached the foyer, he noticed Carrie's luggage sitting in front of the door. He was about to call out to her when she appeared from the rear of the house. She stopped short when she saw him, then forced a smile.

She was already dressed in a pair of neatly pressed pants and a linen blazer. Her hair was pulled back and tied with a scarf that she'd bought in Key West. She looked as beautiful as she had last night, when she'd arched against him in her passion, her eyes dusky with desire, her breath coming in quick gasps.

"Good morning," she said in a quiet voice.

Dev stepped toward her, and almost instantly she took a step back. What was wrong with her? The warm and willing woman who had shared his bed was gone, and he was faced with icy indifference. He watched her for a long moment, then motioned to her luggage. "Where are you going?"

Carrie tipped her chin up as if he had no right to ask. "I'm going home. I'm taking the supply boat back to Key West with the housekeeper's husband in a few minutes. I'll get a flight back to Miami this afternoon."

His jaw tightened and his temper rose. "You were just planning to leave without saying goodbye?"

She gave him a halfhearted shrug. "I'm sorry. I—I didn't want to wake you."

Dev raked his hand through his hair and cursed. "You didn't want to wake me? That's your excuse? Dammit, Carrie, we made love last night. And it was incredible. You don't just sneak off after a night like that."

"I'm sorry," she said.

Dev cursed. "Well, sorry doesn't cut it, sweetheart—no matter how many times you say it. I think I deserve more than just 'sorry.' I deserve an explanation."

He waited for her to speak, refusing to let her off easily. Finally, she looked up from the floor and met his gaze. "You told me that nothing would happen if I didn't want it to. I wanted last night. But I don't want to talk about last night. I just want to leave."

"What is it? Is it that cowboy? Do you feel

guilty? You have nothing to feel guilty about. You haven't betrayed him."

"He's not a cowboy!" she cried in frustration, her fists clenched at her sides. "He's—he's no one. He doesn't make a difference. And I don't feel guilty. That's not why I'm leaving."

"Then stay," Dev said, reaching out for her. "We still have another day here."

She avoided his touch and stepped over to her luggage. "Dev, let's be practical. I—"

"The hell with practical! Why does everything have to be practical with you? We made love last night because we both wanted to. Practicality had nothing to do with it."

"We both knew we'd have to say goodbye sooner or later. I'm making it easier for both of us. I'm just saying that we shouldn't try to make this more than it is—was."

"And what was it?"

Carrie drew a deep breath. "Practice," she said. "I told you why I came here. And you know better than I do that this isn't real. What we shared was a—a fantasy. A vacation fling and nothing more."

Dev laughed bitterly. This is the speech he should be giving her! He'd planned it all out in his head, but now that he was hearing it, he didn't like it at all. "Is that it then? You're just going to walk away." He shook his head in disbelief. He should have known. She was no different than Jillian—just as fickle and coldhearted. What had made him think that she was special?

"Don't make this more difficult than it needs to be," Carrie said, gathering up her luggage. "Let's just leave it as a pleasant memory."

He reached out and grabbed her arm, pulling her to him. "I know you feel something, Carrie. I could see it in your eyes last night. I could sense it in the way you touched me."

"There's nothing," she said. "Nothing that won't go away with time."

Dev's jaw clenched and he tried to rein his temper. Anger would only drive her away. "Carrie, I don't want to forget you. And I don't want you to disappear from my life. Not this way."

"Then what way?" she asked, her question tinged with anger and frustration. "Do you plan to make promises you can't keep? Are you ready to tell me how much you love me? Dev, you don't even know me. You don't know who I am or what I am. We're strangers who shared a bed for a few nights. We don't have to make it mean anything."

But it did mean something to Dev! Until this moment, he hadn't realized how much. He hadn't thought about how he'd feel as he watched her walk away. And now, faced with her departure, he didn't know what to say, how to make her stay. "You're right," he finally said with a shrug. Bitterness welled up inside him, burning away his true feelings. "It didn't mean anything. Go ahead. Leave."

"I don't want you to be angry," Carrie said. "I had a wonderful time this week, and I'm glad I got to spend it with you. I'll never forget it."

"Me, too." With that, Dev picked up her luggage and carried it outside. The housekeeper's husband waited on the terrace. His boat was moored at the dock, waiting to take Carrie away from him.

She stepped out from behind Dev, then took one

final look around. "It's beautiful here. I'm going to miss this place." She glanced over at him and sent him a regretful smile. "Don't worry. You'll forget all about me once you get home." Reaching up, she smoothed her hand over his beard-roughened cheek. "Take care of yourself, Dev Riley."

He turned and placed a kiss in the center of her palm, covering her hand with his. "I don't want you to leave," he murmured.

"I have to."

Dev gazed into her eyes one last time, then nodded. Carrie drew a deep breath, then turned and walked toward the dock. He waited for her to look back, but she never did. She climbed on board the supply boat and stared out at the ocean. He fought the urge to run down to the deck, to pull her off that boat and confess his love for her. To offer her marriage or money or anything that would get her to stay with him.

Dev watched the boat pull away. He watched a woman who he thought he loved sail out of his life for good. A painful emptiness settled around his heart as he realized that he'd never look into her pretty blue eyes again, never touch her soft blond hair and listen to her sweet voice.

Dev braced his shoulder on a pillar and stared out at the sea. "This is not over yet, Carrie. I'm not ready to give you up." He turned on his heel and stalked into the house, then took the stairs two at a time. The boat would be back this afternoon and by then he'd be packed and ready to go.

If his feelings for Carrie had to be tested by the real world, then he better get back to the real world as soon as possible.

8

"I WANT YOU TO PLAN another vacation for me,"
Carrie murmured. "Someplace far away from here.
Someplace where I can forget everything that happened on my last vacation." She stood at the front
door of Adventures, Inc., and looked out through
the frosted glass at the busy main street of Lake
Grove. Winter still held the Chicago area in its grip,
and fresh snow had fallen overnight, turning the
trees white and the streets slick.

She rubbed her arms and remembered the feel of
the Florida sun on her skin, the bone-deep warmth
she had loved, the bright skies and the blue water
and the white sand. Since she'd returned, she
hadn't been able to summon such pure content-
ment again. The weather seemed to hang oppres-
sively over her, as gray and cold as her mood. And
as her tan began to fade, she felt as if she was
slowly losing that person she'd become in the
Keys.

She'd colored her hair back to its mousy brown
and thrown her contacts into a drawer in an attempt to set her life back to rights. But the more she
tried to slip into the day-to-day life of Carrie Reynolds, travel agent, the more she realized that she
couldn't completely go back. She was stuck in

some strange limbo, between the person she'd been and the person she'd almost become.

Now Carrie wasn't sure who she was. All she really knew was that she'd left the best part of herself behind, in that bedroom where she and Dev had made love. Her mind flashed an image of him, lying naked, the sheets twisted around his limbs. She hadn't wanted to leave, but she couldn't face the goodbyes. She didn't want to see the end in his eyes, hear the regret in his voice. They had shared a vacation fling, and though it was wonderful, it couldn't last once exposed to the real world.

But then, she hadn't avoided the most painful part of all. She'd been forced to walk away from him, knowing in her heart that he was the only man she'd ever love. Her fantasy had come to life for one short week, and Carrie had to be satisfied with that. She'd carry the memories of her time with Dev forever. And the next time he came into the agency, her heart wouldn't beat faster and her mind wouldn't spin. She wouldn't gaze at him from afar and let her imagination take flight. Dev Riley was part of her past—and that's where he would stay.

"So, will you plan it for me?" she asked in a soft voice.

Susie sighed, then slipped her arm around Carrie's shoulders. "Running away won't stop you from loving him."

Carrie turned and faced her partner. "Who said I loved him!" she cried. "I never said I loved him." Maybe not out loud, but she'd said it so many times to herself over the past week. She wanted to believe that if the words didn't pass her lips, then the feelings wouldn't be real.

"You loved Dev Riley before you even knew him," Susie said. "Now that you've spent a week with him, you can't tell me that your feelings have changed."

Carrie drew a shaky breath. Susie could always see right through her. She swallowed hard and pushed back the tears that threatened. "I don't know what to do. He'll think I set it all up on purpose, that I went after him. I can't tell him the truth."

"Why not?" her partner asked.

She pressed her forehead against the door and watched as her breath clouded the cold glass. "When he finds out I own the agency that booked his trip, that I live right here in Lake Grove, he's going to think that I tricked him."

"If anyone should feel guilty, it should be me. Not that I do, but I probably should," Susie admitted with a smile. "I'm the one who set this whole thing up. You were completely innocent."

"He's not going to believe that. He told me he loved my honesty. And I'm the biggest liar of all. I could have told him the truth right from the start, from the minute I found myself in the wrong bed, on the wrong vacation."

"Sweetie, why would he be angry? You saw a man you liked and you went after him. He should be flattered."

"That sounds so mercenary. Like big-game hunting. Are the tigers and the elephants flattered?"

"Guys have bigger egos than elephants. I think they like being chased."

"But I didn't go after him," Carrie said, pushing away from the door. "I didn't even like him at first. He was so mean. But then I realized that he was angry because of Jillian. Then he started to be so sweet, and I couldn't help but fall in love with him for real."

"And how does he feel about you?" Susie asked.

Carrie hugged herself and pulled her jacket tighter, shivering despite the warmth of the office. "I'm not sure. We never talked about how we felt. Things just happened between us. We were on vacation. Nobody thinks on vacation."

"So you're going to slip back into your old life? And when Dev Riley comes in, you're going to hide in the copy room?"

"No," Carrie replied. "You're going to start delivering his tickets to his office. I don't have to run into him. Besides, he wouldn't even recognize me if he saw me."

"You didn't have to change your hair. You looked so pretty as a blonde," Susie said.

Carrie shook her head. "It wasn't me. I was pretending to be someone I could never be." She looked down at the drab clothes she wore: the baggy corduroys and the oversize jacket. "This is the real Carrie Reynolds. I'm comfortable with this person. I—I'm happy." She glanced over at Susie. "So, will you plan another vacation for me? Someplace quiet, where I don't have to talk to people."

Susie nodded. "When do you want to leave?"

"I need to catch up on a few things here at the office. I should be ready to leave by the end of the week."

"How long do you want to be gone?" Susie asked.

Carrie sighed and turned to stare out the window. "I don't know. I'll come home when I'm ready."

Susie stepped in front of her and drew her into a hug. "I'm sorry, Carrie. I never meant for you to get hurt."

Carrie rested her chin on her friend's shoulder and distractedly watched a car park across the street. "I know," she murmured. "I know you didn't—" The words died in her throat and she shoved back and glared at Susie. "You did it again!"

Her partner frowned. "What are you talking about?"

Carrie grabbed her hat from a chair and tugged it down over her head. "That!" she said, pointing out the window at the dark BMW sedan. "You knew he was coming here and you didn't warn me. You wanted us to see each other."

Susie shook her head. "I didn't know he was coming! I swear, Carrie, I didn't set this up."

Carrie swung her backpack over her shoulder and grabbed the doorknob. "I have to go. I can't see him. Not yet." With that, she rushed outside. She risked a quick glance across the street, and for an instant, her gaze met Dev's. Then she ducked her head, pulled her collar up and hurried down the sidewalk without looking back.

When she reached a safe distance, she slipped into a shop doorway and tried to catch her breath.

Her heart slammed against her chest and she felt faint. Carrie tipped her head back and cursed softly. "One look," she murmured. "And I can barely walk." She swallowed hard. "I can't do this. I can't risk running into him. I'm going to have to move."

She'd sell her house and start a branch of Adventures, Inc. in another town. Fairbanks, Alaska, or Amarillo, Texas. "Or Helena," Carrie said. "I'll just move to Montana. That would wipe out one lie, at least."

Carrie leaned out and looked down the sidewalk. Dev was just crossing the street, and she watched him. Her fingers twitched as she remembered the feel of his skin beneath her palms, the hard muscle that rippled beneath. For an instant, she was carried back to that room on Cristabel Key—the sea breeze blowing through the shuttered windows, the lazy whir of the ceiling fan, the melodious songs of the birds. She touched her lips and could almost taste his kiss. Every memory was so clear and intense that desire still welled up inside her.

How was she supposed to live without him? How could she go for the rest of her life without ever touching him again? She couldn't imagine feeling this passion for another man. Carrie pressed her mittened hand to her chest, trying to ease the ache in her heart.

There was one way to make things right with Dev. She could walk back into the agency and tell him the truth. Everything. That she'd watched him from afar, that she'd fantasized about him, that she'd deceived him at every turn. And then, once she'd taken in his reaction, she could tell him that she loved him.

"Do it," Carrie murmured to herself. "Tell him the truth. Go to him and ask his forgiveness."

She took a step out from the doorway, and the bitter wind slapped her in the face. In that instant, her courage and resolve vanished. She'd lived a dream with Dev Riley and if she gave him a chance to reject the person she really was, then that dream would be too painful to bear.

Maybe it was better to just leave things as they were, to go back to her life, happy in the knowledge that she'd known one week of true passion. She could live the rest of her days satisfied with that, couldn't she? She could separate the Dev she'd fallen in love with and the Dev that came into her travel agency on occasion.

Carrie turned and headed toward a coffee shop on the next block. She'd wait for a while and then go back to the agency as if he'd never been there, as if she'd never seen him on the street. Or maybe she'd go home and crawl into bed and eat a couple of dozen Twinkies. It was all for the better, keeping her secrets.

And if she told herself that again and again, maybe someday she'd feel it in her heart.

THE FRESH SNOW GLITTERED in the bright noonday sun and drifted with the wind. Dev squinted against the glare as he stepped out of his car across from Adventures, Inc. He shivered and clapped his gloved hands together, waiting for a break in the traffic. After nearly a week in the Keys, it would take more than a day or two in the north to become reaccustomed to the numbing cold and icy wind.

He glanced both ways before crossing the street, then stopped short as his gaze fell on a figure leaving the agency. The woman glanced across the street, and for an instant their eyes met. Then she turned and walked briskly down the sidewalk, her head bent to the wind.

Dev's breath froze in his throat and he blinked against the harsh light. His mind flashed an image of Carrie—her walk, the way she held her head, the easy swing of her arms as she moved. Though the woman wore a heavy coat and a hat, he still felt such a strong sense of familiarity that he took a few steps after her. But then he realized her hair was the wrong color and she wore horn-rimmed glasses.

He stopped his pursuit with a curse and raked his fingers through his hair. Good Lord, he was seeing Carrie Reynolds's likeness in a complete stranger now! Had he become that obsessed with finding her? Had she so totally stolen his heart that he couldn't go a minute without thinking about her?

Since the moment she'd walked away from him that morning at the villa, he'd been assailed by a maelstrom of emotion. He'd been stunned, hurt by her sudden and indifferent departure. Then, he'd grown angry and had managed to convince himself that her leaving was for the best. There'd be no tearful goodbyes, no doubts or regrets, no worries about what might have been. Just a quick and simple end to their vacation affair.

That feeling had lasted all of an hour—as long as

it had taken him to pack and make plane reservations. Then a slow desperation set in, and any thought of forgetting what had happened between them was overcome by a need to find her. What he planned to do once he had her back, he wasn't really sure, but Dev couldn't let her go without seeing her one last time.

He didn't know what he was going to say when they finally came face-to-face. Something would occur to him in the moments before he looked into her eyes. Instinct told him to confess his feelings, to admit that he'd fallen in love with her. But he still couldn't put much faith in such an emotional reaction. They'd known each other for only a week, and love was supposed to take time. He'd agonized over his decision to propose to Jillian after a two-year affair, yet he was now ready to pop the question to Carrie without a second thought.

He wanted to spend his life with her, indulging his fascination with every passing day and every passionate night. They belonged together, in both heart and soul. The fact that he didn't know much about her made no difference. He could learn everything he needed to know to make her happy, and whatever was left, he'd spend a lifetime discovering. Nothing should keep them apart if they truly loved each other.

But there was the rub. He might love her, but did she love him? That was the question that had nagged at his mind during his flight back to Chicago. If she did love him, why did she leave? There was nothing calling her back home, except her love for a man she apparently didn't even know. What would possess a woman to brush aside the experience they'd shared for a relative stranger?

Dev sighed. He really wouldn't get his answers until he found her, which was turning out to be a lot harder than he expected. He'd contacted Fergus and Moira from the villa, assuming that they would have Carrie's home address. But oddly, they listed her hometown as Lake Grove, Illinois, and the agency that booked her trip as Adventures, Inc. Both he and Moira concluded that the bad information was due to another computer glitch.

Left without even the most basic lead, he'd decided to go to Helena. But after a Friday afternoon spent in Carrie's hometown, he was no closer to finding her than he had been in the Keys. Helena wasn't a big place, but short of scanning the phone book and visiting the nine travel agencies in the city, there was nothing more he could do. Carrie Reynolds had disappeared without a trace.

So he'd decided to ask for Susie's help. Dev pushed open the door to Adventures, Inc. and scanned the office for his travel agent. Maybe there was a way Susie could access airline records or track down the reservation that Carrie had made for *Serendipity*. Somewhere out there was another agent who'd made Carrie's arrangements. Maybe Susie could track that person down.

Dev tugged off his gloves and stuffed them in his coat pocket. If Susie couldn't find Carrie, then Dev had only one option left—an option that he was reluctant to employ. His head of corporate security was a former private investigator. Dev had never mixed business with his personal life, but if it came down to it, he'd break his own rules to find her.

"Dev Riley! You're back!"

Dev waved at Susie, then crossed the office and stood in front of her desk. "I'm back."

She pushed back in her chair and gazed up at him. "Sit down," she urged. "Tell me about your trip. I hope everything was as you expected? Very interesting, very relaxing?"

"Very," Dev said. "You planned a perfect trip."

She gave him a sympathetic look. "I'm sorry it wasn't as romantic as you'd planned. I was surprised to hear that your companion decided to cancel. I hope you weren't too lonely."

Dev frowned, then shook his head. There were times when he wondered what his vacation might have been like without Carrie. Even worse, what might have happened had Jillian accompanied him. By now, he could have been an engaged man, promised to a woman he'd never really loved.

But a silly mistake by some travel agent had changed his life, had turned it in a new direction. Maybe fate would prevail, and Susie could do the same all over again. "That's what I wanted to talk to you about," Dev said.

Susie laughed. "About loneliness?"

"No, I wanted to talk to you about a woman. A woman I met on vacation."

"But I thought you were alone," she said.

Dev leaned over her desk and shook his head. "By some strange mistake, *Serendipity* was double-booked. This woman was supposed to go to a singles resort and she ended up on my vacation—in my cabin and in my bed. I wanted to know if there was any way you could track her down. Her reservation was made through a computer service."

Susie blinked in surprise. "In your bed, you say? My, my, you *did* have a good vacation."

"It was wonderful. And that's why I need you to do this for me—why I need to find her."

"You shared a bed with this woman and you didn't bother to get her phone number? Not very good thinking on your part."

"It's not like that," Dev said. "She told me she was from Helena, but I went there and I couldn't find her. You have to help me on this."

"Well, I don't know," Susie said. "I really don't think—"

"You're just about my last hope," Dev said, an edge of frustration in his voice. "Short of hiring a private investigator or putting my corporate security team on her trail."

"You'd do that?" She cupped her chin in her palm and gave him a sly smile. "This woman must be very special."

"She is," Dev replied. "I've never met anyone quite like her."

"How special?"

He didn't anticipate having to explain his motives or his feelings about Carrie Reynolds to his travel agent, but he was depending on Susie's help. "I think I love her," he said. Once the words were out of his mouth, he suddenly didn't question his feelings. "I do love her," he corrected. "I know it sounds silly. I mean, I never put much stock in love at first sight. But then, when it happens, well…"

"Well? Well, what?" Susie asked.

"Well, it's pretty incredible. So that's why I need you to track this woman down."

"So tell me," Susie teased, "is she beautiful? Let

me guess. Tall, slender—a brunette with an attitude?"

"Not even close," Dev said with a smile. "She's small and not skinny. Curvy, just perfect. And she's blond with blue eyes. The most incredible blue eyes. And the sweetest smile."

"Doesn't sound like your type," Susie commented, leaning back in her chair.

"That's what I thought. But I guess I really didn't know what my type was until I met her. So, can you find her? I thought you might be able to check airline records."

"I can try," Susie said. "Why don't you give me a day or two and I'll get back to you?"

Dev nodded, then met her gaze squarely. "This is very important to me. *She's* important. I have to find her." He stood and rebuttoned his overcoat, then shook Susie's hand. "Let me know as soon as you find anything."

With that, he turned and strode out of the agency. When he got to his car, he sat behind the wheel for a long time, his breath clouding around his face and fogging the windows. Something nagged at his brain, something he'd forgotten. But Dev couldn't put his finger on it.

And then he remembered! He'd never even mentioned Carrie's name to Susie Ellis. And she hadn't even asked for it. He grabbed the door handle and pushed the car door open. How was Susie supposed to track Carrie down if she didn't know who she was looking for? Unless, she could get her name off the computer reservation on *Serendipity*.

Still, Dev wasn't willing to take any chances. He stepped out of the car and quickly ran across the street and into the agency. But by the time he got there, Susie was already occupied with another client. Dev tried to catch her attention, but she was too absorbed in her work to see him. Finally, he walked over to another agent.

"I'm wondering if you could give Susie a message," he said. "I don't want to disturb her when she's with a customer."

The agent looked up from her computer and smiled. "Sure," she said, grabbing a message pad and a pen. "What would you like me to tell her?"

"Tell her that I want her to find Carrie Reynolds."

"Oh, Carrie was in just this morning. In fact, she just called to say she'd be back in later this afternoon. Would you like to make an appointment?"

"No, no," Dev said. "Susie is looking for Carrie Reynolds for me. She doesn't work here. She's from Montana."

"Oh, no, Carrie is from right here in Lake Grove. She and Susie own the agency."

Dev shook his head, trying to make sense of the woman's words. Carrie Reynolds worked here, at the agency? But how could that be? Why would she have told him she was from—

Realization slowly dawned, and suddenly Dev understood everything quite clearly. There was no computer error with Carrie's reservation. It had been made from here at this very agency. And no wonder he couldn't find her in Helena. She didn't live in Montana, she lived in Lake Grove, Illinois! She'd come on his vacation, knowing full well who he was. Yet she'd kept her identity a secret.

Dev frowned. Those were probably the facts, but

he was missing one very important bit of information—why? What had she hoped to accomplish by barging into his vacation? Surely Susie must have known, but why had *she* played coy with him? Were the two of them scheming in some way? He rubbed his forehead, trying to soothe away his confusion. "You say Carrie Reynolds will be in later this afternoon?"

The agent nodded. "She always closes. She's usually here until six-thirty or seven to handle the after-work walk-ins. Would you like an appointment?"

"No, I just think I'll stop by and see if she's free. Is Susie scheduled to work that late?"

The woman checked her computer, then shook her head. "Not tonight. Carrie will be the only one here. If you want to see Susie, she's got a one o'clock slot open."

Dev nodded. "No, I'd really like to talk to Ms. Reynolds." He pushed to his feet. "Thank you for all your help. It's been quite...illuminating."

The agent smiled brightly. "No problem," she chirped. "Have a nice day."

With that, Dev turned and headed back out the door. Oh, he'd have a nice day all right. And he'd have a nice week and a nice month and a nice life. Just as soon as he figured out what the hell was going on!

CARRIE STARED at her computer screen, comparing prices on first-class flights to San Francisco. A group tour of the California wine country for a local senior citizen's group had kept her busy for most of the evening, ticketing and making rooming lists. The tour was being led by a local wine merchant who'd promised colorful commentary on vineyards and wine-making.

She was tempted to go along, just to get away from Lake Grove and any chance of running into Dev Riley again. Moving was out of the question. Carrie had decided that earlier in the afternoon between the Twinkies and the Ben and Jerry's. She'd just have to learn to live with what might happen. And if she couldn't, then there was always the option of clearing the air with Dev. She could tell him the truth, and take her knocks. And after that, she could put her life back together and go on.

With a soft sigh, she went back to her ticketing. The front door squeaked, then slammed shut, and Carrie looked up from her task. Her heart froze in her chest, and a strangled cry worked its way out of her throat, as she watched Dev Riley stride toward her desk. Frantic, she searched for a place to run, a spot to hide—anywhere to get away from him.

Finally, she slipped down to the floor and crawled beneath her desk, hoping against hope that he hadn't seen her. From where she hid, she could see his feet, his expensive Italian shoes and argyle socks. He looked so different in a business suit and tie—not at all like the man she'd made love to. He was more imposing, more intimidating. She wished he were dressed the way he had been in the Keys: in shorts and a T-shirt. Carrie could talk to that man, but she couldn't talk to the stranger who'd walked into her travel agency.

"Hello?"

She decided to keep quiet, hoping he'd just go away.

"I can see you under there," he said. "Hello? Are you all right?"

"Hello," Carrie called. "I—I'm perfectly fine. Can I help you?"

He braced his hands on her desk and leaned over until Carrie could see the top of his head. She scrambled farther beneath the desk.

"I was looking for Susie," he said. "Is she in?"

Carrie coughed softly, trying to clear away the nerves in her voice. "No, no, she's not. She'll be in tomorrow. You can come back then."

His feet slowly circled around to the back of the desk, and soon she could see all the way up to his knees. He had nice knees, she remembered. And wonderfully long and muscular legs. In her mind flashed a memory of him walking from the surf, naked, his body glistening in the moonlight.

"What are you doing under there?"

Startled out of her brief fantasy, she sat up and bumped her head on the underside of her desk. With a soft oath, she rubbed the spot. "My pencil. I dropped my pencil."

Dev pulled a pencil from the cup next to her computer and held it out to her. "Here's a pencil."

"No, I want the pencil I dropped," Carrie said. "It's a...special pencil."

"Well, when you find it, will you come up here and talk to me?"

"I thought you wanted to see Susie. She's not here. If you leave and come back tomorrow, I'm sure she'll help you then."

"I'll settle for you."

"I'm afraid I don't have time," she called.

"You have time to search for a pencil you don't need, but you don't have time to help a customer?"

Carrie groaned inwardly. He wasn't going to go away. He'd stand over her desk and badger her until she came out. But as soon as he looked into her eyes, he'd surely recognize her. Drawing a deep breath, she slowly wiggled out. The choice had been made. There'd be no avoiding the truth now. She'd be forced to tell him everything. But maybe that was for the best. Maybe fate had stepped in to make the decision for her.

She hesitantly straightened, brushed off her corduroys, then looked up at him. Carrie expected an immediate reaction—recognition, surprise, confusion. But Dev simply stared at her with an impatient expression. She swallowed convulsively. Could it be that he didn't recognize her?

"Did you find your pencil?" he asked.

Carrie shook her head and quickly sat down, tugging her hair down to hide her face. He *didn't* recognize her! Her glasses had effectively hidden her eyes, and her hair was no longer a sunny blond. Still, she'd spent an entire week with the man—even made love to him! He'd seen her at very close range. How could he *not* recognize her?

She wasn't sure whether to feel relieved or insulted. He'd claimed that he'd never forget her, yet they'd been apart for two days and he couldn't recall the features of her face or the sound of her voice. Carrie ground her teeth. It would serve him right if she told him exactly who she was! Let him try to squirm out of *that* one.

Carrie opened her mouth—ready to speak her

mind—then snapped it shut. Did she really want to explain her actions? Did she want to admit that she'd fallen in love with him over a year ago, before she'd even met him? That all her daydreams had come true when she'd found him in her bed on *Serendipity?* Because that's what she'd have to tell him if she told the truth. There were no other explanations.

"What can I help you with, Mr...."

"Riley," he said. "Dev Riley."

"Mr. Dev Riley." Lord, she loved the sound of his name on her lips. It had run through her head a million times since she'd been home, but saying his name out loud caused her heart to skip and her pulse to quicken.

"Susie was working on a project for me," Dev explained. "Maybe she told you about it?"

"I'm afraid I haven't talked to Susie since this morning. But I'm sure I can help you with any arrangement that you'd like made."

"Actually, I'm looking for a woman."

Carrie stared up at him and blinked in surprise. "A woman?"

Well, it certainly hadn't taken him long to get on with his life! They'd barely been apart for forty-eight hours, and he was already on the make. Oh, she was so much better off without him. And she was so relieved she hadn't revealed her identity. How humiliating would that have been?

"Her name is Carrie Reynolds," Dev said.

She gasped, all the breath leaving her lungs. "Carrie Reynolds?"

"I met her on vacation in the Keys. And I've been

trying to track her down ever since. Susie was trying to help me find her."

"Susie knows that you're looking for—this woman?" She'd nearly said "me," but caught herself just in time. "You discussed this with her?"

"I talked to her earlier today. She's looking at airline records and computer reservation services to try to track her down."

Oh, Lord. Dev Riley was looking for her! Maybe he did care, maybe he regretted letting her walk away. Maybe he even loved her. Or maybe he wanted to see her for another reason. She recalled his description of his breakup with Jillian: how he had wanted to be the one to end it. Could that be why he searched for her? So he could reject her the same way she'd rejected him?

"I—I don't think she'll be able to find much," Carrie said. "Airline records are confidential." She paused. "Why do you want to find this woman?"

His eyebrow shot up, and he looked insulted by her prying inquiry.

"I mean, you're not a stalker, are you?"

"We left some things unsaid," he replied.

"Like what?"

Dev frowned and shook his head. "That's between me and Ms. Reynolds, don't you think?"

Carrie felt a flush creep up her cheeks, and she ducked her head down, worried that he might recognize that particular trait of hers. She had blushed a number of times in Dev Riley's presence. One in particular came to mind—when he'd come upon her on the terrace steps...when she'd asked him to make love to her.

"Of course it is," she said. "I just thought that—"

"That I'd confide in a complete stranger?"

He slid his hip onto the corner of her desk, and her gaze fell to his lap, to thoughts entirely inappropriate at the moment. "I'm not a complete stranger," she murmured, her embarrassment rising. "I mean, I'm Susie's partner. You can tell me anything."

He scowled at her. "I don't know much about her. She ended up in my cabin on a charter sailboat. Some mix-up with the reservations. Over the week we spent together, we became...close."

"Close?"

"I don't think I need to go into detail," he said. "She claimed she was from Helena, Montana. I went there to look for her and she—"

Carrie twisted her fingers together in an attempt to contain her surprise. "You went to Helena? To look for—her?"

"As I said, it's imperative that I find her. I'm prepared to pay you for your time."

"You'd *pay* to find her?"

He pushed to his feet. "Whatever it takes. I'm not going to stop until I see her again. Do you understand, Ms.—"

"I understand, Mr. Riley. And I can assure you that we'll try our best."

"I don't want you to try, I want you to succeed," he said. With that, he buttoned his overcoat and tugged on his leather gloves. Then he walked to the door and stepped out into the night, leaving her alone and completely baffled.

Carrie rubbed her forehead. If he cared for her, why hadn't he recognized her? She yanked open her desk drawer and rummaged for a pocket mirror. She finally found an old compact in Susie's desk and flipped it open. "I don't look that different," she murmured, pulling her hair back from her face. "It's me—the same person he taught to swim, the person he kissed and made love to. If he cares enough to find me, then why can't he remember me?"

Unless...Carrie winced. Unless he really didn't care. Maybe all he wanted was to vent his anger, to settle some imagined slight. He could want to hurt her in the same way she'd hurt him.

Carrie plopped down in her chair and covered her eyes with her hands. How had this turned into such a mess? Dev was determined to find her, and, considering his financial resources, it wouldn't be long before he turned up here again, looking for answers.

Well, she wasn't about to wait in fear. She'd give him the answers he wanted right now! Carrie sat up in her chair and typed in a few commands on her computer. In an instant, she had Dev's client profile, a list of every trip they'd ever booked for him and his home address. She scribbled the address on a scrap of paper, then grabbed her jacket from the back of her chair and headed for the front door.

The weather had turned nasty since she'd arrived at the agency. Flurries had turned to a full-fledged snowstorm. The wind whipped the flakes into drifts on the streets. Carrie trudged down the sidewalk, squinting against the snow that clung to her hair and her lashes.

Dev lived in an old neighborhood on the edge of Lake Grove—a spot filled with beautiful brick homes and large yards. She could walk the distance, or she could go home and get her car. Carrie decided that she could probably cover the mile faster on foot, considering the condition of the streets. Besides, walking would give her the chance to figure out exactly what she wanted to say to Dev Riley. She had an unfortunate tendency to talk without thinking first around Dev. If ever there was a time she needed to have her wits about her, it was now, when the fate of her future and Dev's was about to be sealed.

9

THE WIND RAGED OUTSIDE and snow pelted the windows of Dev's study. He poked at the fire he'd built to ward off the chill, then sipped at his scotch. As the liquor traced a line of fire down his throat, his mind drifted back an hour, to the very moment he'd set eyes on Carrie again. A flood of desire welled up inside him even now.

He might not have recognized her had he passed her on the street, but face-to-face, he knew her in a second. She'd changed her hair color to an unremarkable shade of brown, and she now wore glasses. But the eyes behind the glasses were undoubtedly the same eyes that had gazed into his when they'd made love.

Dev wasn't sure what he'd hoped to accomplish by confronting her at the travel agency. Maybe he hoped she'd explain how—and why—she'd ended up on his vacation and in his bed. And why she'd walked out on him with barely a goodbye. But she hadn't even admitted that she was Carrie Reynolds!

So he'd decided to play along with her charade. There had to be a good reason for her subterfuge. Maybe there was another man—or a husband. An unbidden flood of jealousy shot through him, and he pushed it back with another swallow of his scotch. Wouldn't that be his luck, to find a woman he loved and to lose her to someone else?

He'd have his explanations soon enough. First, he'd wait to hear Susie Ellis's story: the results of her "search" for a woman who wasn't lost. And perhaps he'd pay another evening visit to the agency to test Carrie's nerves. Or maybe he'd run into her on the street and—

As Dev stared into the fire, watching the flames lick at the birch logs, a spark popped onto the hearth, red and glowing, then faded, and with it came a memory, just as quick and fleeting. That hair, those eyes. He had seen her on the street earlier in the day! The woman he'd noticed, with Carrie's walk, the tilt of her head. That had been her, leaving the agency.

Bracing his hand on the mantel, he closed his eyes and tried to picture the scene. How had she ever expected to keep her true identity from him? He visited Adventures, Inc. at least once a month to pick up tickets or make travel arrangements. And he and Carrie lived in the same town. For all he knew, they had run into each other many times before—in the post office, at the grocery store, at the train station.

The grandfather clock in the hall struck seven, and he downed the rest of his scotch. He needed some dinner before he sat down to catch up on all the work he'd missed. But as he headed for the kitchen, the doorbell rang. Dev frowned. Who would be out on a night like this? He peeked out the window at the shadowy form before he flipped on the outside light and opened the door.

A figure, bundled in a jacket, muffler and hat, stood on his porch. The person had snow stuck to every exposed surface like some Arctic explorer. He leaned closer and watched as the woman blinked her eyes, the only indication that she wasn't frozen solid. Beautiful blue eyes behind half-frosted glasses. "Carrie?"

She nodded, then shuddered with the cold. Dev grabbed her mittened hand and drew her into the house. The door slammed closed behind her, and he carefully began to remove her wet clothes. Layer by layer, the clothes and the snow fell onto the marble floor of the foyer, until Carrie was standing in front of him, her hair damp and her cheeks red.

He removed her glasses, wiped the fog from them with the cuff of his shirt, then returned them. "What the hell are you doing out on a night like tonight?"

Carrie's teeth chattered, and she stared up at him, wide-eyed. "You—you recognize me? You know who I am?"

"Of course I do," he said. He grabbed her hand and pulled her toward the study. "There's a fire in here. Let's get you warm. "

"You know who I am," she repeated, stumbling along after him. "And you're not surprised to see me?

"Stop saying that. Yes, I know exactly who you are."

"But—but you were at the agency earlier. You walked right in and started talking to me as if you didn't know me. Did you know who I was then?"

Her questions were beginning to irritate him, and he ground his teeth. "Why do you think I was there? I came to see you."

Suddenly, she dug her heels into the oriental carpet and yanked her hand from his. "What kind of game are you playing?"

Dev turned to her, meeting her angry gaze. "I could ask you the same," he said in a deceptively even voice. "Don't you think I'm the one who deserves an explanation, Carrie? You told me you were from Montana. And here you are in Lake Grove. Living here, working here, right under my nose. And that's just the first of your lies."

"It's not like that!" Carrie said, crossing to the fire. She held out her trembling hands, then rubbed them together distractedly. He wanted to press her fingers between his, to draw them up against his chest and warm them against his body, but he clenched his fists at his sides and waited. Waited for her explanation. But she seemed intent on studying the flames.

"I suspect I know what the real story is," he said. "You and Susie saw an easy mark. A guy who'd just been dumped by his girlfriend. A guy with a little money, a business of his own and—"

"That's not it!" she cried. "I would never do that! How—how could you even think I'd be capable of something so…devious?"

A long silence grew between them. "You showed up at my door," he said softly. "You obviously came here for a reason. What was it?"

She pressed her lips together, as if she needed to contain her emotions. The fire cast her beautiful profile in light and shadow, and he couldn't take his eyes off her. "I came to explain." Her voice was so small and soft that he could barely hear her.

"I'm listening."

She still refused to turn and look at him. Dev stepped up beside her and she gave him a sideways glance, then turned back to the fire, as if looking at him made her explanations harder. "Remember when we were talking about the prom?"

"The prom?"

"You said you would have taken me to the prom if you'd known me in high school. That you would have noticed a girl like me. And I said I wasn't the kind of woman men noticed."

"I remember."

"Did you know that we met once?" she asked, glancing at him again. "Before the Keys. On the street in front of the agency. I slipped and fell on the ice, and you helped me up."

That's why he'd felt a spark of recognition when he'd first seen her on *Serendipity*. They had met and he'd remembered her—vaguely. "That was you? With the backpack and the grape juice?"

Carrie nodded, then stepped away from the fire and rubbed her arms. She took a seat on the leather couch and shoved her glasses up the bridge of her nose, then hugged her knees to her chest. Dev almost felt sorry for her. She looked so timid, not at all like the bright and confident woman he'd met in the Keys. He wanted her angry or frustrated or hysterical. He didn't want her quiet and complacent.

"Can you still say the same?" she asked, meeting

his gaze. "Look at me. Can you honestly say that you would have noticed me? Would have been attracted enough to ask me out?" She held up her hand. "You don't have to answer. Those were rhetorical questions."

"I'll answer," Dev said. "No, I wouldn't have noticed you. And I wouldn't have asked you out. But then, I rarely take much notice of strangers, and I never ask them out. But we got to know each other in Florida and that changed everything. I got to know you, Carrie, and I—"

"That wasn't me," she interrupted. She pressed her palms to her heart. "This is me. This is Carrie Reynolds. I'm shy and quiet and plain. I live in Lake Grove, and I own Adventures, Inc. And—and..."

"And what?"

She fixed her gaze on her tightly clasped hands. "And I've been in love with you for a long time. At least, I thought it was love. I didn't know what love was, so I guess you could call it a crush."

"A crush?"

A long breath escaped her tightly pursed lips. "You'd come into the agency, and I'd watch you from the copy room, or sometimes from my desk. You never noticed me. I used to think you were the most handsome, most interesting man in the world. You were everything I thought I wanted... and everything I knew I could never have."

"So you—"

She held up her hand to stop him. "Don't say anything. Not until I've told you the whole story."

Carrie took another deep breath and continued. "For a long time, I kept my feelings secret. I thought they were silly...childish. But then Susie noticed me watching you and she realized what was going on. She took matters into her own hands and she sent me on that vacation, knowing that you would be there and Jillian wouldn't."

"Susie did all this?"

"The travel arrangements. But I could have told you the truth when you arrived. I could have left for home after that first night. But I stayed. And I kept up the lie." She sniffled, then wiped her damp nose on the cuff of her sweater. "I—I just thought you'd think I'd set it all up, to trap you or manipulate you or whatever it is women do when they see a man they want. Until you turned up in my bed, you were just a fantasy. I never meant for it to be anything more. I never meant it to be real."

He stared at her for a long time, confusion addling his brain. He didn't know what to say. Dev ran his hands through his hair and let out a tightly held breath. "Then it was real?"

She shook her head, then quickly stood up. "No. It was a fantasy, and now that fantasy is over." Carrie forced a smile. "I just wanted to clear the air. I'm terribly embarrassed about what happened. I never wanted it to go so far and I shouldn't have let it. You deserved the truth." Carrie turned on her heel and started out of the study. In three long steps, he caught up to her and grabbed her hand.

"Where are you going?"

"Home," she murmured in a tremulous voice.

"I've said what I came to say, and now I can leave."

The hell if he was going to let her walk out of his life for a second time! "You can't leave," he said. "The storm is worse. And your jacket is all wet. It's too cold for you to walk home."

"I'll be all right," she said, hurrying back to the foyer. "Please, I've already humiliated myself enough for one night. Don't make it worse. Just let me go."

"What if I don't want to let you go? What if I can't?" Dev asked, following after her.

She looked back and into his eyes, pain etching her beautiful features. "You have to. We're back in the real world now, and there's no room for fantasies." She laughed softly. "Look at me. And look at you. We don't belong together. Never in a million years would you have come to me on your own. We met through a manipulation—a silly joke that a friend decided to play."

Dev wasn't sure what to say. On one hand, he was angry—about the lies, the scheming, her complicity in the whole thing. On the other hand, he ought to be flattered. She'd fallen in love with him without ever knowing—

"I'm the cowboy," he said, realization slowly dawning. "I'm the guy you were practicing for?"

Carrie nodded, two spots of color deepening on her cheeks. "I thought if I were more interesting, more confident...more experienced, that I might have a chance with you—with men. I went on vacation to practice."

"So the whole time it was happening between

us, I was thinking you were in love with another man. And you were getting exactly what you wanted."

"I never meant to hurt you." She grabbed her jacket from the floor and tugged it on. "I was selfish. After a while I couldn't tell you the truth, even when I knew you might get hurt." She zipped up her jacket. "You didn't get hurt, did you? I mean, you're all right. I can tell you are. You'll be fine."

"I will?"

"You haven't lost anything. You were getting a woman who doesn't really exist, at least not outside the Florida Keys. This is the real Carrie Reynolds," she said.

"I don't see any difference," he said. "You've changed your hair, you're wearing glasses, but you're still the same woman I met on *Serendipity*."

Carrie shook her head. "No, I'm not. And I'm honest enough to realize that." She tugged her hat down over her ears, then wrapped her scarf around her neck. "Now that I've told you, I think I should be going." She swallowed hard, then forced a smile. "I really hope this doesn't jeopardize our business relationship, but I'll understand if you decide to work with another agency."

Dev cursed beneath his breath. After all this, she was concerned about keeping his business? What about the passion they'd shared? What about the need and desire he'd felt while holding her in his arms? Was she so immune to those feelings that she could turn and walk away from him? Hell, she was no different from Jillian!

Dev slowly shook his head as he stared at her, realizing she was right. The Carrie Reynolds standing in front of him *was* different. This wasn't the woman he'd fallen in love with—the silly, clumsy, smart-mouthed woman who drove him mad with desire. "Maybe you're right," he murmured.

Pain flashed in her eyes, and he saw her lower lip tremble. "I knew you'd realize that I'm not the woman you want—the woman you need."

Dev sighed. "I'm not sure what I need right now."

"Maybe you need things to get back to normal. What we shared in Florida was—nice, but it's over. You can go back to your life, and I can go back to mine." She paused, then held out her hand. "Goodbye, Dev."

He took her fingers in his, ignoring the current that shot up his arm and twisted at his heart. "Goodbye, Carrie."

With that, she turned and walked out of his home. Dev stood at the front door for a long time, the snow blowing in around him, the wind chilling him to his core. He wanted to run after her, to convince her that they could recapture what they'd shared in the Keys. But he wasn't sure she cared about him enough to make that happen. Or that she cared about herself enough to allow it to happen.

In all honesty, Dev wasn't sure about anything anymore. Except that he was in big trouble. For he was more in love than ever with Carrie Reynolds.

"YOU DIDN'T TELL ME why Dev came to the agency! And you didn't tell me that you told him who I was!"

Carrie stood in the middle of Susie's kitchen, dripping melted snow on her shiny linoleum floor. It had taken her nearly an hour to walk from Dev's place to Susie's apartment, fighting the snow and the wind and her tears the entire way. Colder and wetter than she'd ever been in her life, Carrie longed for the warmth of the Key West sun, the feel of the soft ocean breeze on her face. Right now, she felt like a drowned rat—a half-frozen, emotionally spent, heartsick drowned rat.

Susie sat at her kitchen table, munching on a handful of potato chips as she gazed up at Carrie. "I didn't tell him anything. And I didn't say anything to you because you said you wanted to put him out of your mind. Isn't that what you said?"

Carrie ripped off her mittens and threw them on the floor, where they landed with a splat. "I know that's what I said, but I expected you to tell me if he mentioned me to you."

"Run that by me again?"

"You know what I mean." She unwound her scarf. "He came into the agency looking for me. Looking for Carrie Reynolds."

"Umm-hmm," Susie said. "He's desperate to find you. He asked for my help, and if I don't help him, he's going to hire a private detective to track you down. Isn't that romantic?"

"Well, he asked for *my* help in tracking me down, too. When he came in, he was looking for you. But he knew he'd find me."

"This is really confusing," Susie said, crinkling

her nose and picking at the potato chips. "Besides, I didn't tell him where you were."

"He already knew! He was playing a game with me, hoping I'd admit the whole story."

"Why would he play games with you?" Susie asked, leaning back in her chair. "He loves you."

Carrie gripped the edge of the table with cold-numbed hands. "What? What did you say?"

"I said, he loves you."

"He said that? Dev said that he loved me?" She pulled the chair out and sat down. "He said those exact words?"

"Sure. Right out loud, right there in our office. Why else would he be so crazy to find you?"

Carrie combed her fingers through her wet hair. "I don't know. He didn't really say. I thought he wanted to get even. I thought he might be mad about what happened. So I went to his house and told him everything."

"Everything?"

"After all I said—humiliating myself that way—he just let me walk out. He didn't say anything about love. He must have lied to you." Her breath caught in her throat, and a stab of regret pierced her heart. "Or maybe, after seeing me, he changed his mind."

Susie reached across the table and covered Carrie's icy fingers with hers. "What did you say to him?"

A lump of emotion clogged Carrie's throat. "I told him everything. About the crush and the fantasies, about how I've loved him for a long time. And then I told him that we didn't have a future together," she said, rubbing her cold face with her hands. "I was giving him an easy way out. And he took it."

"You were avoiding rejection again," Susie said. "Only this time, you ran away from a guy who wasn't planning to reject you."

"He can't love me!" Carrie cried. "Not really. Look at me. How could he love someone like me? He thought he loved me, but now he doesn't. I was right all along."

With a frustrated sigh, Susie pushed up from her chair and grabbed Carrie by the hand. "Come with me," she said, dragging her to the bathroom. She flipped on the light, pushed Carrie in front of the mirror, and pointed at her reflection. "Look at you. Don't look at the details—the stringy hair and the red nose. Look at the total picture, Carrie. You're pretty. And you're just about the sweetest person I know. You'd never say anything bad about anybody. You know how to keep a secret. And you're loyal to your friends. And even you have to admit that you're funny. Why wouldn't he love you?"

Carrie stared long and hard at herself. Maybe Susie was right. She wasn't that unattractive, even with her mousy brown hair. And though her figure didn't come close to super-model status, she looked like a real woman, with curves in all the proper places. "But he's so...worldly. Experienced. Sophisticated."

Susie reached up and pulled Carrie's damp hair away from her face. "Terrific guys fall in love just the same as ordinary guys. And they fall in love with terrific women—just like you."

"He loves me?" Carrie murmured. "He really said that?"

"He loves you," Susie replied. "And I don't think seeing you again, even in this condition, changed his mind at all."

"But why did he let me leave?"

"Maybe because he thought you didn't share his feelings," Susie suggested.

Carrie turned and hurried out of the bathroom. "I have to go home. I have to think about this. I told him that we didn't have a future. I thought I was making things better...easier. Why didn't he tell me how he felt?"

Susie dragged her back into the bathroom. "Sweetie, we've got ourselves a blizzard here and you're already freezing. Why don't you get out of those wet clothes, take a nice hot shower, and I'll go get you some pajamas. We can have a slumber party. And we can talk about Dev and what you plan to do." Susie plucked at Carrie's hair and winced. "And maybe we can color your hair. This just doesn't do a thing for you."

Carrie slapped her hand away. "I like my hair just the way it is. It's me."

Her friend's eyebrow arched. "It would be you if you were a rodent living in a hole in the wall. This is not a color meant for a woman's head."

The mirror revealed the truth in Susie's words and Carrie sighed. "It isn't very pretty, is it?"

Susie smiled. "I'll run out to the drugstore and get everything we need. What do you think. Honey blond? You could go red. Or a pretty brunette.

New hair will give you a completely new outlook on life—and love."

"Changing my hair color isn't going to solve all my problems."

"Maybe it will make you remember what's really important. Who you *really* are. And after we color your hair, we can talk about you and Dev and what you're going to do. We'll get it all sorted out, you'll sleep on it, and tomorrow morning you'll know exactly what to say to him to get him back."

"I'm not sure I can do anything," Carrie replied.

"You're going to have to talk to him again. You can't let him go on thinking you don't care. He loves you, Carrie! This is a big deal." Susie grabbed her around the neck and gave her a hug. "Of course, I'll be your maid of honor, as long as you don't make me wear one of those frilly dresses."

"No! I mean, there won't be any dresses, frilly or otherwise. We're not going to get married. He doesn't want to get married—not after Jillian."

Susie reached into the tub and turned on the water. "Take a hot shower. Then we'll color your hair, polish your fingernails and eat a lot of junk food. Things always seem clearer after a junk food binge. I'll bring you pajamas, and then I'll run to the drugstore." She patted Carrie's back. "We're going to figure this out before the night is over."

After Susie closed the bathroom door behind her, Carrie slowly stripped out of her damp clothes, her body numb. A shiver skittered down her spine, not from the cold but from the raw emotion that raced through her. Dev Riley loved her. But why hadn't he told her? He'd admitted as much to Susie, but he hadn't said the words to Carrie.

Would he say it again, if she gave him the chance? Could he put everything she'd said to him aside and reveal his true feelings? She'd tried her very best to convince him that she was a different person from the one he'd made love to at the villa. Maybe she'd tried too hard and had banished every bit of love from his heart.

Carrie stepped beneath the hot water, letting it wash over her body until it began to warm her blood. Her eyes closed, and exhaustion nearly overwhelmed her. Just a little more than a week ago, she might have described her life as normal— a little boring, but nothing out of the ordinary. Suddenly, everything she'd come to depend on had been thrown into chaos, and all because of Dev Riley. Nothing had prepared her for the power of her feelings, or the possibility he might return those feelings. What was she supposed to do? Could she trust his love? Or would he fall out of love, the way he had with Jillian?

Another stab of pain wretched her heart. She'd dreamed about loving him for so long, and now he'd professed to return those feelings. But would they last, or was he still infatuated with the woman Carrie had been? Carrie couldn't face the thought that she might lose him as quickly as she had found him. There were no guarantees they'd spend the rest of their lives together just because he claimed to love her now.

Bracing her hands on the tile wall of the shower, Carrie bent her head and let the water run along her spine. She couldn't work this all out in a few minutes or even a few hours. She needed time to think, time to weigh the risks of letting herself love Dev Riley—and of letting Dev Riley love her.

Carrie had always assumed that if—or when—she finally found love, it would all be clear to her. But it wasn't at all. Love was confusing and exhilarating and frightening and comforting. It stood before her like a wonderful dream that she was afraid would dissolve in the blink of an eye, as soon as she reached for it.

Closing her eyes, she turned her face up into the spray. Why couldn't she just grab that dream? She deserved to be happy, didn't she? "I'll take my time and think this over," she murmured. "And when I wake up in the morning, I'll decide what to do. If Dev truly loves me now, then he'll still love me tomorrow."

CARRIE SHOVED HER CARRY-ON into the overhead bin and wrestled a pillow and blanket out at the same time. She glanced around the first-class cabin at the other passengers, then sat down in her seat. Susie's seat next to her was empty, and Carrie wondered where her partner was. They'd planned to meet at the gate, but when she hadn't arrived by boarding time, Carrie had decided to wait on the plane.

When Susie had suggested they take a little junket, Carrie had jumped at the chance. After almost a week of mulling over her options, she had finally worked up the courage to call Dev. But he'd been out of town for the entire week, and his secretary refused to say when he'd be back.

Carrie couldn't help but feel relieved. She wasn't sure what she'd planned to say to him. Perhaps she might have been better prepared had she experienced love before. But Carrie had never been in love—not even close. All the emotions that spun inside her were completely new and unfamiliar.

How was she supposed to make a decision about something so serious, so life altering, without any understanding of what she felt? Time should have been her ally, each day crystalizing her feelings, until her decision was clear. But the longer she waited, the more she doubted herself—and doubted Dev's love.

She'd hoped that he might make the first move, make things easier on her. But obviously, he hadn't felt any urgency—he'd left town! All week, she'd waited for the memories of him to lose their intensity, to fade with each passing day. Maybe if she never saw him again, the images would someday disappear altogether. But it would take a very long time.

Carrie leaned back in her seat and sighed, hugging the little pillow against her chest. She needed to see him again, longed to look into his eyes, to reassure herself that he still wanted her. A girl just didn't toss aside a man like Dev, or procrastinate so long that he lost interest. She'd have to do something—soon!

A shadow fell across Susie's seat and a briefcase dropped down next to Carrie. "I'm afraid that seat is taken," she said, glancing up.

"I sure hope not. Because you're in *my* seat."

Carrie's heart stopped as she looked into Dev Riley's eyes. He slipped in beside her and tucked his briefcase beneath the seat in front of him. "First my bed and now my seat," he said. "I never considered you the desperate type, but this is getting a little out of hand, don't you think?"

"Wha—what are you doing here?" she demanded, heat rising in her cheeks.

"I'm taking a little trip," Dev replied. "And I'd assume you're here to tag along again?"

Carrie stood up and bumped her head on the overhead bins. She searched up and down the aisle. "Where's Susie? That's her seat, not yours."

"Oh, she's not coming. It's just you and me."

Carrie cursed softly. "I can't believe she's done this to me again. I didn't plan this. I didn't know you'd be here. And—and I'm not desperate!" She scrambled over him, out into the aisle, then grabbed her bag from above her head, nearly knocking him unconscious in the process. "I want to get off!" Carrie called to the flight attendant.

The attendant hurried toward her. "Ma'am, you can't get off. We've already closed the doors."

"Then open them. I can't stay on this plane."

She patted Carrie on the shoulder. "Please take your seat, ma'am. We're starting to pull back from the gate."

Carrie hefted her bag up and tried to push past the fight attendant. "Listen, sister, I'm a travel agent, and if you don't let me off this plane, I'm never going to book your airline again!"

"And if you don't sit down and fasten your seatbelt," the attendant said in an even voice, "I'm going to have to call the pilot. Now, please, take your seat!"

"I think you better do as she says. Threatening a flight attendant is a federal offense." Carrie glanced down to see Dev still smiling at her. He patted the seat beside him. "I'll let you have the window seat."

Carrie scowled, then reluctantly crawled over his legs and sat down beside him. "I'm going to kill Susie. How could she do this to me again? Aren't you angry?"

Dev buckled his seatbelt and cinched it tight, then leaned back and closed his eyes. "Susie didn't do this, I did."

Carrie gasped. "What?"

He opened one eye and then the other. "I figured if I was going to talk to you, I needed to get you alone first. There were no sailboats handy, so I took the next best thing. You can't get away from me on a plane—unless you have a parachute. You don't have a parachute in that bag of yours, do you?"

"I don't want to talk to you," she said.

"Too bad. We've got a four-hour flight and we are going to straighten this whole mess out. I was hoping you'd come to see me again, but—"

"I called your office, but you weren't there."

Dev blinked in surprise. "I never got the message."

"That's because I didn't leave one."

"Well, then, you can see why I had to resort to—"

"Kidnapping?" she finished.

"Not even close. You have a ticket for this flight, and you got on board of your own free will. Nobody forced you."

"I thought I was going on vacation with Susie."

"You *are* going on vacation. With me."

Carrie jumped up from her seat, but the flight attendant gave her a warning glare, and she sat back down again. "I—I can't go on vacation with you!"

"And why not? We spent a lovely time together in the Keys. We make good traveling companions. You do like traveling with me, don't you, Carrie?"

She narrowed her eyes. "Oh, you're exactly the kind of man a woman would want to spend her vacation with," she shot back in a sarcastic tone. "You're arrogant and selfish and egotistical and—"

"Now there's the Carrie that I know and love," he said with a soft chuckle. "I knew I'd find her in there somewhere, if I just pushed."

Her heart lurched at his simple confession. *The Carrie he knew and loved?* Over the past week, she'd dreamed of him saying those words, admitting his feelings for her. He reached out and tried to grab her hand, but she pulled it away. "I forgot to add *manipulative* to the list of your attributes," she murmured weakly, her indignation slowly dissolving.

Dev shook his head. "Carrie, what are you so afraid of? My feelings are perfectly clear, but I don't have a clue as to how you feel. Tell me so I can sort this mess out."

She turned and stared out the window, watching as the plane taxied to the runway. What was she supposed to say? She didn't know what frightened her, or why she was so reluctant. Putting her feelings into words had only brought a mass of confusion and doubt. But she had to try. This was her chance to make things right with Dev. Maybe her last chance.

"I'm afraid because I don't know what I'm doing," she murmured. She looked at him and forced a wavering smile. "I've never been in love before. I'm afraid I'll make a mistake, and then you won't love me anymore."

"That's not going to happen," he said, his words so resolute that she could almost believe him.

"How can you be so sure? You don't know me, Dev. I've been living my whole life afraid of rejection. One offhand comment from you, and I'll start doubting myself again. I'll start doubting your... love. I don't know if I can be the kind of woman you want."

"I think that's my decision, don't you?"

"You don't know me, Dev! How can you love someone you don't know?"

"I know that Carrie Reynolds is not two different people. Our vacation in the Keys was the first time in your life you got a chance to be the real you. You let go of your past and responsibilities and all your worries—and someone very special came out. That's you, Carrie. And so is that bedraggled woman who showed up at my door the other night. And the woman with the sunburned face. And the woman I made love to at the villa. They're all you, and I love them all."

"How can you be sure?"

Dev shrugged and smiled. "I just know." He

took her hand and pressed it to his heart. "I know it in here."

Carrie could feel his heart beating, strong and sure, as certain as the words he'd said. Then she pressed her other hand to her own heart. Her pulse raced and jumped.

"Just where did you get the idea you're not allowed to be happy?" he asked in a soft voice. "Have you spent so much time taking care of other people, you feel you don't deserve to have a good life? Maybe no one has ever told you that you should have the best. I'm telling you now. You deserve all the happiness the world can offer."

The plane began to accelerate, and Carrie closed her eyes and clutched at the armrests with bloodless fingers. Everything was out of her control. She couldn't stop her love for Dev anymore than she could stop the plane from hurtling down the runway and rising into the sky.

She swallowed hard and her ears popped. Higher and higher they flew, the roar of the jet rumbling in her head. But then Dev silently laced his fingers through hers and kissed her wrist. Suddenly, all the fear evaporated from her mind and her body—fear of the future, of rejection, even of flying. In one single instant, she felt completely safe. Just from a simple kiss.

If his kiss could make her feel this way, what could a lifetime with Dev Riley accomplish? She did deserve to be happy! To be loved and cherished. He was offering her a real life, with passion and joy and excitement filling every day and night. And she'd been too afraid to reach out and grab it.

Carrie drew a deep breath and opened her eyes. All the very best things in life came at a risk, didn't they? But if she spent all her time protecting her heart, then she'd never be able to truly love anyone. And she wanted to love Dev Riley, so desperately. She wanted to give her heart to him completely.

The seat-belt bell sounded. She glanced over at Dev and found him staring at her. Everything he felt for her was mirrored in those green depths and in his warm smile. A wave of confidence washed over her, and she stood up. "Come with me," she said.

He stepped out of his seat. "Where are we going? We're on a plane."

"We need some privacy," she said as she moved out into the aisle. She pulled him toward the bathroom at the rear of the first-class compartment. To her relief, it was unoccupied. Carrie opened the door and stepped inside, then dragged him after her. The door clicked shut behind him.

Airplane bathrooms were too small even for one person, and she found herself pressed up against Dev's body. He grinned and wrapped his arms around her waist. "We're alone now. What did you want to say?"

"It's what I want *you* to say," Carrie replied. "Tell me. Tell me how you feel."

He bent down and pressed his forehead against hers, gazing into her eyes. "I love you, Carrie Reynolds. I'm not sure when I fell in love with you, but I know my feelings aren't going to go away. Not in this lifetime." He paused and brushed his lips against hers in a sweet, but fleeting kiss. "I don't care how long I have to wait. I'll wait forever for you if I have to. But I want you to know, I'll never hurt you, and if you—"

"And I love you," Carrie said. "I thought I loved you before I even knew you. But now I realize that wasn't really love. This is love—what I feel in my heart right now. This is real."

A slow grin curled his lips. "You do love me?"

Carrie nodded. "I don't know what took me so long to say that. To truly believe it. I was just so afraid, so confused." She shook her head. "When Susie sent me on vacation, she promised me I'd come back a whole new person. And when I did, I wasn't sure what to do. I didn't know how to deal with the new Carrie Reynolds or all the feelings that she was having for you."

"And now you do?"

She wrapped her arms around Dev's neck and pushed up on her toes to kiss him long and hard. "I want you in my bed, Dev Riley. Not just for a week, but for the rest of our lives. I want to wake up with you every morning and go to sleep with you every night."

Dev spanned her waist with his hands and pulled her up against him, laughing softly. "Just think. All of this because you ended up in the wrong bed."

"*You* ended up in the wrong bed," Carrie teased. "That bed was mine."

"Well, I want you in the right bed from now on. My bed."

"Our bed," she corrected.

"Our bed," he agreed. He kissed her again, and this time, Carrie surrendered completely to him.

She had wanted an adventure in her life—exotic travel, exciting new places, glamorous people. She had wanted to be more interesting, more sophisticated—the kind of woman a man like Dev could desire.

It wasn't until this very moment, here in this rest room high in the sky, that Carrie realized adventure wasn't just found in the world around her—on planes and boats, in foreign locales and luxury hotels. Adventure was found in her heart and deep in her soul. And in the overwhelming love she felt for Dev.

She pulled back and gazed up into his eyes—eyes that were filled with all the love he felt. Carrie tipped her head back and laughed. If she knew anything about Dev Riley, she knew the greatest adventure of her life was about to begin right now.

If you enjoyed what you just read,
then we've got an offer you can't resist!

Take 2 bestselling
love stories FREE!

Plus get a FREE surprise gift!

Clip this page and mail it to Harlequin Reader Service®

IN U.S.A.	IN CANADA
3010 Walden Ave.	P.O. Box 609
P.O. Box 1867	Fort Erie, Ontario
Buffalo, N.Y. 14240-1867	L2A 5X3

YES! Please send me 2 free Harlequin Temptation® novels and my free surprise gift. Then send me 4 brand-new novels every month, which I will receive months before they're available in stores. In the U.S.A., bill me at the bargain price of $3.12 plus 25¢ delivery per book and applicable sales tax, if any*. In Canada, bill me at the bargain price of $3.57 plus 25¢ delivery per book and applicable taxes**. That's the complete price and a savings of over 10% off the cover prices—what a great deal! I understand that accepting the 2 free books and gift places me under no obligation ever to buy any books. I can always return a shipment and cancel at any time. Even if I never buy another book from Harlequin, the 2 free books and gift are mine to keep forever. So why not take us up on our invitation. You'll be glad you did!

142 HEN CNEV
342 HEN CNEW

Name	(PLEASE PRINT)	
Address	Apt.#	
City	State/Prov.	Zip/Postal Code

* Terms and prices subject to change without notice. Sales tax applicable in N.Y.
** Canadian residents will be charged applicable provincial taxes and GST.
  All orders subject to approval. Offer limited to one per household.
  ® are registered trademarks of Harlequin Enterprises Limited.

TEMP99   ©1998 Harlequin Enterprises Limited

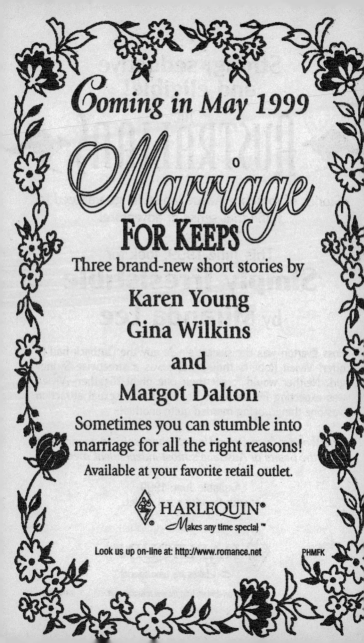

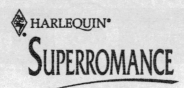

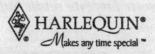

COMING NEXT MONTH

#733 ONE WILD WEEKEND Rita Clay Estrada
Bachelor Auction

Buying time with renowned photographer Archer was
Melody Chase's last chance. She needed to know how to land a
man, and who better qualified to tell her than someone who
spent his life dealing with desirable women? The problem was,
Archer decided he wanted Melody for himself...for only one
wild weekend.

#734 SEXY AS SIN Meg Lacey

When Chastity Goodwin saw sexy Sin O'Connor roar up to her
door on a motorcycle, she knew she was in for a fight. No way
was this man going to willingly replace his black leather and
denim for a doublet and tights—not even for his brother's
wedding! But Sin was full of surprises. And willing to take off
his clothes...as long as Chastity did, too.

#735 WHILE HE WAS SLEEPING Carolyn Andrews
The Wrong Bed

Hopeless romantic Daisy Hanover wasn't looking forward to
her upcoming marriage of convenience. So when she discovered
a quaint country inn, boasting a bed that promised wedded bliss
to the couple who shared it, Daisy made arrangements for her
fiancé to meet her. After one night, Daisy definitely found bliss.
Only, the man in her bed *wasn't* her fiancé!

#736 BRAZEN Carly Phillips
Blaze

After agreeing to a loveless marriage, Samantha Reed decided
to run away for a week and experience a lifetime's worth of
passion—even if it was with a stranger! Sexy bartender
Ryan "Mac" Mackenzie seemed like the perfect man to love and
leave behind. Only, Mac wasn't a bartender—and he wasn't
letting Samantha go anywhere....